2:32AM

Losing faith in God

2:32AM

Copyright ©2018 Lakisha Johnson

Published by Lakisha Johnson | Twins Write 2 Publishing

All rights reserved.

Edition License Notes

This book is licensed for your personal enjoyment only. This book may not be re-sold or given away to other people. If you would like to share this book with another person, please purchase an additional copy for each recipient.

If you're reading this book and did not purchase it, or it was not purchased for your enjoyment only, then please return to your favorite retailer and purchase your own copy. Thank you for respecting the hard work of this author.

2:32AM

Dedication

This book is dedicated to my niece ...

Makaela Antoniece Rucker

September 21, 1996 – November 29, 1996

God loaned her to us for 2 months and 8 days and although we miss her, we will never forget her!

2:32AM

My Gratefulness

As always, it is to God whom I owe everything. If it wasn't for the gift He so graciously etched within me, I wouldn't be able to do what I love. To write and encourage.

To my husband, Willie, my children Gabrielle and Christopher; thank you for sharing a piece of me with the world. I love you!

To my sister, Laquisha, who supports me and who took the time to read this book, before anybody else; knowing it would dredge up memories; THANK YOU and I love you!

And to every one of you, who support Lakisha, a huge THANK YOU, GRACIAS, MERCI, GRAZE and ARIGATO!

This means thank you in English, Spanish, French, Italian and Japanese.

I would not be the author I am without readers like you. It is because of you purchasing, reading, reviewing and recommending that pushes me to be greater with each release. Thank you from the bottom of my heart!

2:32AM

2:32AM

Losing faith in God

2:32AM

Charlotte

"Charlotte, baby, what's wrong?"

"Huh?"

"What's wrong, you're moaning."

I open my eyes to look at him.

"Huh? I asked him again because I didn't know what he was talking about.

"Are you okay? You were moaning in your sleep." He says.

I jolt up from the bed and look at the clock.

2:32am.

I touch my breast because they were so full of milk and were hurting. I look at him again, a little confused.

"Did you feed the baby?"

"No why?" He ask turning back over.

2:32AM

"She's normally up to eat by now."

"Babe, if she isn't crying that must be a good thing. Lay back down."

"I need to check on her."

"Charlotte, leave her alone and let her sleep."

I get out of bed and I have to use the bathroom but getting to her was the only thing on my mind. I walk over to her crib and she's laying there, on her back.

The same way she was when I laid her down two hours ago.

I let out the breath I was holding but I look at her again.

Something is different.

I touch her but she doesn't move. I grab her hand and my heart starts beating fast.

"KEITH! I scream picking her up. KEITH!"

When he gets to the door, still half asleep, I look at him and it feels like I'm speaking but no words are coming out.

"Charlotte, what?"

"SHE.IS.NOT.BREATHING!" *I mouthed in slow breaths.* "SHE IS NOT BREATHING! DO SOMETHING!"

"Oh my God. No, please don't leave me. Please!"

"Charlotte. Charlotte, look at me."

I open my eyes to look at Dr. Mitchell. "Take a breath."

"Oh God, this hurts so badly." I cry, cradling her blanket in my hands.

"I know but we will get through it."

"Why do I have to relive that night?"

"Charlotte, it is the only way for you to face your pain."

"But retelling it makes it worse." I tell her.

"I know but it's only for your good." Dr. Mitchell says. "Let's end our session for now and we can pick up again in our next meeting."

I nod.

"Do you have enough sleeping pills?"

"Yes."

"Are you taking them?" She asks.

I nod.

"Good because you need to sleep. If you don't, I'm going to put you on a 72 hour hold. Do you hear me?"

"Yes, I hear you." I say grabbing my things and stuffing the blanket in my purse.

"Can we pray before you leave?"

"Not today," I tell her. "I will see you Thursday."

I walk out of her office to Keith waiting for me.

"Hey, are you okay?" He asks when he looks into my face.

"Yeah."

"How was it?"

"The same as always, painful."

"Babe, I know you don't like talking about what happened but you need to."

"Why Keith? Why do I need to relive that night over and over with a complete stranger?"

"So you can deal with it."

"And how are you dealing with it?"

2:32AM

He doesn't answer, instead he walks over and opens the door to let me in the car. Once he gets in, he turns to me.

"Babe, I'm just worried about you."

"I'm fine."

"No you're not. If you were fine, I wouldn't keep finding you in the nursery every morning at 2:30."

"2:32."

"What?"

"2:32 is the time I found her."

He sighs.

"Why won't you talk to me Charlotte?"

"I don't want to hear the pity in your voice."

"This isn't pity, its pain. A pain we're both feeling but you will not let me in. Charlotte, I'm hurting too."

"You didn't find her."

"I know but it doesn't mean I am hurting any less. Just let me help you, hold you, pray with you; something."

"Pray? What is prayer going to do? If God was going to do anything, He should have saved our baby."

"Don't talk like that. You as well as I know the bible says, the Lord gives and the Lord takes away."

"Well, I don't want to hear it. Save it for church on Sunday."

"Char--"

"Keith, please. I am tired and just want to go home."

"Would you at least eat something?"

"Maybe later."

2:32AM

Keith

"THE.BABY!"

I walk over to where Charlotte is standing and take the baby from her arms. I look into her face to see her lips are blue. I touch her hands and they are cold.

"Charlotte, call 911."

She doesn't move.

"CHARLOTTE, CALL 911!" I scream as I place her on the floor to begin CPR.

"Come on baby, breathe. Breathe for daddy, please."

Charlotte leaves and comes back, a few minutes later with the phone gripped to her chest.

"Did you call?"

She doesn't respond.

"Charlotte, come on, I need you to answer me. Did you call?"

She nods yes.

"Good. Now, go turn off the alarm and open the door."

She doesn't move, her eyes are fixated on the baby.

"Charlotte, come on baby, I need you to help me!"

She still doesn't move.

I start to do CPR again until I hear the sirens.

"Baby, I know this is hard but I need you to go and let the paramedics in. CHARLOTTE!" She jumps at the sound of my voice. "Please baby, go turn off the alarm and open the door."

A few seconds later, the EMTs run in.

"Sir, what happened?" One of them asks taking over, moving me out of the way.

"I don't know. My wife found her."

2:32AM

"Ma'am, can you tell us what happened?" They ask Charlotte but she doesn't respond.

"Where was she found?"

"Her crib." I say.

They spend a few minutes trying to shock her, in between performing CPR before they stop. One of them walks off, talking on his radio and the other comes over to me.

"Sir, can you take your wife out of the room?"

"What about my baby?" I ask. "Why are you stopping?"

"I'm sorry sir." He says looking down. "She's gone."

I jump up, wiping the sweat from my head. I reach over and as usual, the side of the bed, where my wife should be is cold. I look at the clock and see it is 2:45am.

I throw back the covers and make the usual steps across the hall. Pushing back the door, I see Charlotte sitting in the rocking chair.

She's singing.

"Lord, keep me day by day. In a pure and perfect way. I want to live, I want to live on, in a building not made by hand. Every day I pray, Lord keep me day by day. In a pure and perfect way. Lord yes, I want to live, I want to live on. Oh, in a building not made by hand."

"Charlotte."

"I'm okay Keith. You don't have to keep watching me like I'll slit my wrist at any moment. I'm hurting, not suicidal."

"I was only going to ask what you were singing."

"A song by LeAndria Johnson." She says reaching over to stop the music playing on her phone.

I sit on the floor in front of her.

"It's been a while since I've heard you sing."

"I didn't have a reason too."

I don't say anything.

"I never would have thought we'd be here." She says. "Never in a million years."

I place my hand on her leg and for the first time, in months, she doesn't push me away.

"Keith, I am so sorry for shutting you out. I know this has been just as hard on you as it is on me. Please forgive me."

"Baby, there is nothing to forgive you for. You, we; are grieving and it is natural to push people away."

"I know but not you. While I was sitting here, I realized how much we need each other and I cannot imagine losing you too."

"I'm not going anywhere. Will you please come to bed?"

"I will, in a minute. I just want to sit here a little while longer but you go ahead."

I get up but then I stop.

"Charlotte, I know you haven't been praying lately but will you allow me to pray with you now?"

"I'm not ready Keith. Just give me some time."

"I love you Charlotte Hulbert and we will get through this."

"I love you too."

I walk back into our bedroom but before I get back in bed, I kneel beside it.

"Father God, as I petition your throne, I first thank you. Thank you for your grace and your mercy that has been keeping us. Thank you for covering our minds and for your shield of protection that has kept us safe during our grief. Heavenly Father, we don't know what tomorrow holds but we are trusting in you. Continue to strengthen my wife while you use me to be what

2:32AM

she needs. And God, I know I don't have to ask but please take care of our baby girl until we see her again on the other side of glory. This prayer I ask, in your name. Amen."

Charlotte

"I sit in the middle of the floor, cradling the cold body of my baby girl, begging her to wake up. Keith tells me for maybe the fifth time, it's time to let her go but I wasn't ready. I didn't think I could ever let her go. I look up at him and he knew what my eyes were saying because he told me I had to, so I did."

I stop talking because I could feel the anger building.

"Why would God do this? It's not fair." I cry, pulling my arms closer to me. "It's not fair."

"Okay Charlotte, let's take a break." Dr. Mitchell says breaking my thoughts.

"Dr. Mitchell, what good is this doing? You have me recalling one of the most difficult times of my life. Why?"

2:32AM

"Charlotte, when you find the strength to talk about it, you find the strength to overcome it. Tell me about her memorial service."

I get up and walk over to the window.

"The day was warm. She was buried on Sunday, April 16, a week after she died. It was small, just immediate family. I stood beside her small pink and white casket for what seemed like forever. My eyes were covered by shades but they didn't stop the tears. I wanted so bad to reach in and get my baby but I knew she was gone. I can still hear the pastor's voice."

I touch my ear.

"Our Father in heaven, we come this afternoon to thank you for the precious life of baby Micaela. We know God you are the giver and taker of life so we dare not question your will. We only ask you keep watch over her until she shall meet her parents again. Guide the hearts of this weeping

mother and father, comfort them in their lonely hours and give them strength when their thoughts seek to drown them. Let them know, God, this is not their fault but your will. In your name we pray. Amen."

"Forasmuch as it hath pleased Almighty God of His great mercy to take unto himself the soul of this blessed baby girl, we therefore commit her body to the ground; earth to earth, ashes to ashes and dust to dust. As Jesus, during his earthly life, took the children into His arms and blessed them, may you, Jesus Christ, receive this dear one unto yourself, in sure and certain hope of the Resurrection to eternal life, through our Lord Jesus Christ; who shall change our vile body, that it may be like unto his glorious body, according to the mighty working, whereby he is able to subdue all things to himself. Amen."

2:32AM

"When he was done, Keith and I placed a flower on her casket and then we left."

I wipe the tears and turn back to Dr. Mitchell.

"Have you been back to her grave?"

"No, not yet. I will one day but I'm not ready because I may not leave it."

"How often do you say her name?"

"Not often enough."

"What was her name Charlotte?"

"Micaela Olivia."

"Why Micaela Olivia?"

"Micaela means gift from God and Oliver is Keith's middle name." I chuckle a little.

"Why did you laugh?"

"It's funny to think we named her because she was our gift from God yet He took her."

"Do you find yourself mad at God?" She asks.

"More than you can even imagine. I sometimes find myself wanting to ask him why He would give her to us for ninety-six days but then I don't."

"Would it make a difference?"

I look at her.

"Think about it? If you had the chance to question God on why He took what belongs to Him, would His answer make a difference?"

"I guess not but being mad at Him is the only way I know to deal with this. Every time I look at the crib, she did not get to use, I get angry. Keith and I are faithful in our church and this happened to us. He's a deacon and I sing in the choir, we pay our tithes and teach Sunday school. This wasn't supposed to happen to us."

"What makes you exempt from suffering Charlotte? Do you not understand we all have a share in this thing? Yes it hurts and sometimes your suffering may be harder than mine but it's necessary."

"Losing my baby girl was necessary? For who?"

"What I mean is, suffering is necessary." She clarifies.

"Yea, well it still doesn't make it any easier."

"What can? Alcohol can't, drugs can't and you know for sure, being mad at God can't."

"What else am I supposed to do then?" I say angrier than I meant too.

"Okay, let's end for today. Would you like to pray before you leave?"

"Not today. I will see you on next week."

I get to the car and I sit there for a minute before I start to drive, only to end up at the cemetery.

My phone rings causing me to jump. I press the answer button on the steering wheel.

"Hey babe, how was your therapy session today?"

"Same as always."

"Are you on the way home?"

"Yea, I'll be there in about 30 minutes."

"Are you okay?"

"I'm fine Keith. I'll see you in a bit."

"Okay. I love you."

"I love you too."

2:32AM

Keith

I hang up and watch Charlotte as she sits in her car. She didn't see me because I was leaving the cemetery, when she was pulling in. I park, where she can't see me and wait.

When she pulls off, without getting out, I am a little disappointed but all I can do is pray she finds the courage soon. I lay my head on the back of the seat and close my eyes.

"Oh my God! Oh my God!"

"Babe, what's wrong?" I asks running into the bathroom. "Charlotte, what's wrong?"

She turns to face me with tears streaming down.

"What?" I ask again. "Babe, talk to me."

"We're pregnant."

"We're pregnant? Are you sure?"

She shows me the test.

"YES!" *I scream, grabbing her in a bear hug before kissing all over her face. "We're going to have a baby."*

The sound of my phone brings me out of my thoughts. The day we found out we were pregnant is ranked as one of the happiest days of my life.

My phone vibrates again.

"This is Keith." I say when the Bluetooth connects.

"Where are you? I need to talk to you."

"Not right now, I'm headed home to check on my wife."

"Keith, I am tired of begging you to talk. Either you meet me or I'm coming to your house."

"Why can't this wait? It cannot be that important."

2:32AM

"How do you know when you keep dodging me?"

"I'm not dodging you."

"Whatever! Are you coming or not?" She asks.

"Where are you?"

"Pulling up at home."

"Meet me at the park down the block."

"Why can't you come to my place? It's not like you haven't been there before."

"Look, either meet me at the park or stop calling."

I end the call and hit the steering wheel.

Twenty minutes later, I turn in and park a few cars down from hers and get out. I tap on the passenger side window for her to unlock the door.

"What's so important it couldn't wait?"

"Why are you being so mean to me all of a sudden?"

"I am not being mean but we both know what happened between us was a mistake. I was in a weak place, mentally and you were there. Not to mention the drinking."

"So, it didn't mean anything to you? I was just a way to relieve stress?"

"Look, I don't mean to discount your feelings but you cannot sit here and tell me you are okay with this?"

"I am not okay with how it happened but I am happy it did."

"Are you serious?"

"Very." She smiles.

"I don't know what you hope will come of this but what we did will not happen again. I love my wife and these past few weeks have been the hardest of our life."

"What about me Keith?"

"What about you?"

"What am I supposed to do about my feelings for you?"

"I suggest you swallow them and move on."

"Wow."

"You cannot tell me you're shocked at this? We were both drunk and grieving. It doesn't take away the fact I slept with you but I will not make that mistake again."

"I was just a mistake?" She asks crying just as my phone rings.

"Hold up." I say answering the phone. "Hey babe, you okay?"

"Yeah but I'm stopping by to see my parents before I go home. I didn't want you to worry."

"Okay. I'll see you when you get there. Give them my love."

I end the call and slide the phone into my pocket.

"I've got to go."

"Keith wait, I love you."

"What?"

"I love you and I don't want to lose you."

"Lose me? You never had me."

"You cannot just throw me away like I'm nothing. That night, what we shared was special."

"No, what we shared was stupid and I was stupid for turning to you when I should have been consoling my wife."

"But she pushed you away. If anyone is to blame here, it's her."

"She was hurting. We'd just buried our daughter. You know this!"

"Yes and I also know instead of being with her, the night of the memorial, you were with me. I was the one consoling you, not her!"

2:32AM

"What do you want from me?"

"I want you to end things with her and be with me."

"I am not going to do that."

"Then I'm going to tell her."

"Don't do this."

"Why not? I don't have anything to lose."

"She's your best friend Dakota. You cannot do this."

"Well, you should have thought of that."

Charlotte

I make it home and Keith still hasn't made it. I stopped and picked up some hot pineapple fried rice and pad Thai noodles from this Thai restaurant Keith and I love.

I put the food on the stove while I go shower and change into some shorts and tank.

Walking down the hall, I hear the chirp of the alarm.

"Keith?"

"Hey baby, you picked up food?"

"Yea, I thought we could have dinner together since it's been a while."

"I'd like that. Do I have time for a quick shower?"

"Sure."

2:32AM

I hear my phone vibrating on the table.

"Hey." I say putting the phone on speaker.

"Hey girl, I was calling to check on you. How are you?"

"I'm good. How are you?"

"Same."

"I haven't seen you since the night of the memorial service, is everything okay?"

"Yea, I've been busy with work and I knew you and Keith would need space to deal with everything. Anyway, what are you up too? Want to get out and grab some dinner?" She asks.

"I actually picked up dinner for us tonight, I'm just waiting on him to get out the shower. But are you sure everything is okay?"

"Yea, everything is good. Maybe a raincheck, lunch next week?"

"That sounds great."

"Okay, what about Tuesday?"

"Make it after one and I'll be there."

"Our usual?"

"Zaxby's." We both say together before laughing.

"It's good to hear you laugh Charlotte."

"It feels good to laugh. Thank you Dakota and I'll see you Tuesday."

"Who was that?" Keith asks walking into the kitchen.

"Dakota. We're meeting for lunch on next week."

"Oh."

"Oh what?"

"Nothing, I'm just glad you're getting out. Speaking of getting out, you want to come to prayer meeting with me tonight?"

"No, maybe next week."

2:32AM

"Babe, you cannot keep shutting God out. We need Him."

"Keith please don't start. All I need right now is food."

He sighs.

"Look, I am not shutting God out but I am angry at Him and I need to deal with this my way. Okay?"

"Okay."

After we eat, Keith leaves headed to church. I clean up the kitchen and finally change clothes before I decide to catch up on some TV. Getting settled on the couch, I press the power button and wouldn't you know it, the TV is on the Word Network.

"Really God?" I ask out loud.

"The bible shares in Romans 8:18, yet what we suffer now is nothing compared to the glory he will reveal to us later. That's the word of God for the people of God." The TV Evangelist declares. "Do you believe it? For our present troubles are small and won't last very long! Why? Because they produce for us a glory that vastly outweighs them——"

I turn the TV off.

"Small? My present suffering isn't small when it feels like it is hard to breathe. My present suffering is heavy and it hurts. Do you hear me God?" I scream. "My present suffering is heavy and it hurts!"

I throw the blanket back and begin to pace in the living room.

"Why did this have to happen to us? Why my baby? Why did you give her to me for only 96 days? I didn't even have a chance to love her good. Why God?"

"Charlotte."

I jump at hearing Keith's voice.

2:32AM

"Why would God do this?"

He walks over to me and I back up.

"Baby, stop pushing me away. Let me hold you."

"I don't want you to hold me, I want to hold her."

"I know but she's gone."

"It's not fair."

I allow him to get closer before I collapse in his arms.

I jump up and realize I'm in the bed, still fully dressed. I hear Keith snoring beside me, so I slip out. Looking at my watch, it's a little after two.

I pull our bedroom door closed before stopping to use the hall bathroom. I don't know why but I go and grab my laptop before walking into the nursery.

I rub my hand over the crib's rails before pushing the curtains back, to let the moonlight in. I sit on the floor, with my back against the wall and wait until the computer powers on. When it does, I click onto wordpress.com.

I fill in all of the information to start a new blog. I look at my watch again and I wait. When it reaches the correct time, I begin typing.

2:32AM | May 19, 2017

Blog Title: 39 Days

It's 2:32AM and I don't know why I am up. That's a lie. I'm up because it has been exactly 39 days since I found our baby girl dead in her crib.

At 2:32AM.

SIDS or Sudden Infant Death Syndrome.

This is what the medical examiner said took her.

And I thought we were being careful. My husband and I read all of the books, we took all of the precautions and she still died.

Why am I sharing this? I don't know. Maybe it's easier to share with complete strangers than it is to continually hold it in.

IT HURTS!

Her name was Micaela Olivia and she was beautiful. She was our blessing, our rainbow baby or a baby born after miscarriage.

Yep. I had her after suffering two miscarriages and God still took her. My therapist ask me, every time I see her, if I am angry at God.

Shouldn't I be? Isn't it natural?

Everybody wants me to pray to Him but I'm not ready to forgive Him yet. I will eventually but I'm just not there right now. Don't get me wrong, I still trust God but I'm mad at Him.

Am I not entitled?

Anyway, I'm going to sign out for tonight. Maybe someone will read my personal thoughts and maybe they won't but it feels good to get them out.

Until next time.

Char.

2:32AM

Keith

Walking to my car in the parking garage, for lunch, someone clears their throat.

"Dakota, what are you doing here?" I ask looking around.

"I've been calling you for over three weeks."

"I asked you to stop."

"There's something we need to talk about."

"Look Dakota--"

"I'm pregnant." She blurts.

"Congratulations."

"By you."

I take a step back as I try to recall that night.

"Oh, you may not remember the details of our blessed night but I sure do. So, congratulations baby daddy." She says walking up to me.

"No, this cannot be happening."

"It's a blessing."

She reaches in to kiss me and …

"Keith?"

I turn at the sound of Charlotte's voice.

"What in the hell is going on?"

I push Dakota away.

"Baby, it's not what it looks like."

"It looks like you were about to kiss my best friend so I am going to ask for the second time, what is going on?"

"I'm pregnant. By Keith." Dakota sings.

Charlotte drops the bag of food, she was holding.

2:32AM

"Wait," she says laughing. "Girl, I thought I heard you say something crazy. Whew, it must be my emotions."

"Charlotte, I'm pregnant and it's Keith's." She repeats, matter-of-factly.

I run over to Charlotte.

"Baby, please let me explain."

"Have you been sleeping with my best friend?"

"Look, we didn't mean for this to happen." Dakota says walking over to us.

"Is she speaking for you now?" Charlotte ask snatching her arm from me.

"Babe--"

The words don't fully leave my mouth before she turns back and slaps me across the face. She then moves to Dakota who backs up.

"Oh, don't worry, I have no plans on putting my hands on you but let me tell you something.

You are an evil, malicious piece of a woman and I pray God has mercy on your soul."

"I'm sorry Charlotte but maybe this is a blessing."

"The only thing you are right about is you being sorry because you are one sorry best friend. You had the nerve to call, like you were really worried about me. I ought to punch—you aren't even worth it. Lose my number. Matter of fact, act like I'm dead to you."

"Charlotte wait!" I try to run after her but Dakota grabs my arm.

"Keith!" Dakota yells.

"Leave me the hell alone. Do not call me again!" I say jumping into my car to follow my wife.

She pulls up at home and I park behind her to keep her from leaving. She gets out and doesn't say anything before going into the house.

2:32AM

I run in behind her and she is pacing in the living room.

"How long? How long have you been sleeping with my best friend?"

"Baby--"

"Don't call me that just answer my question."

"It only happened once."

"When?"

I drop my head.

"WHEN KEITH!"

"The night of Micaela's memorial."

"Wow." She says as tears stream down her face. "Out of all the women in Memphis, you had to choose my best friend. What is wrong with you?"

"I didn't mean for this to happen."

"What a lame excuse. How could you not mean to sleep with my best friend? MY BEST FRIEND!"

"That night, I was so lost. You wouldn't talk to me, you kept pushing me away. It felt like I was losing you too."

"So this is my fault?"

"No, this is all on me but what I'm trying to explain is, I was in a dark place. You'd taken some sleeping pills and cried yourself to sleep. Dakota was still here helping me clean. We started drinking and--"

"Not only did you sleep with her but you did it in our house?"

"We were out in the back yard."

"Oh, that makes it better." She says sarcastically, wiping her face.

"Please don't cry, I didn't mean to hurt you."

"These tears are not because of you, they are to keep me from killing you right now."

"I'm sorry Charlotte."

"You expect your empty apology to fix this? She's pregnant Keith, with your baby and I just buried mine. What in the hell am I supposed to do? Huh? Are you even thinking about how I feel right now? You need to leave!"

"Please don't ask me to leave, we can work this out. Baby, we need each other."

"Did you think about that before you stuck your penis inside of my best friend? Did you ever stop to think about your wife whose grief is twice as hard as yours?"

"How could I when you wouldn't let me in?"

"Did you ever stop to think my not speaking to you wasn't personal but it was hard for me to put my feelings into words? Did you ever think maybe I pushed you away because I felt like I let you down by not saving our daughter and I couldn't stand to see the pity in your eyes? Did you ever once consider me?"

The reality of her words cut me to the soul. I open my mouth but no words come out.

"Keith, these last few weeks have been the roughest weeks of my life. Every morning, at 2:32, it feels like I relive the night of finding Micaela over and over again. This pain has pierced a part of me I didn't even know existed. Yes, I may have pushed you away but all I needed was time."

She pauses but then continues.

"Even while my breasts still hurt from making milk for a baby I cannot nurse, I still get up, every day, trying to survive. Even when I forget for a moment and walk into her nursery, I'm still right here. RIGHT HERE! Standing, trying to reclaim my life. I apologize if I handled the grief of the miscarriages and Micaela differently than you but I would have never cheated on you and broken our vows."

2:32AM

She turns and walks away from me. I follow her into the kitchen where she grabs a bottle of water.

"Charlotte, I am so sorry."

She doesn't say anything.

I watch as she takes her migraine medicine. When she walks out the kitchen, I don't follow. I stand there until I hear the door to our bedroom close.

I walk back into the living room and fall down on my knees, in front of the couch.

2:32AM | May 31, 2017

Blog Title: Grief

It's 2:32am and again I find myself up. This morning though, it's with a hand full of sleeping pills and a glass of wine.

As I recount, over and over, the thirteen pills (thirteen is what I have left in the bottle), I've contemplated swallowing them.

One by one.

But I'm not.

Sure, I've weighed the options of life on earth versus eternal rest but who is to say one is better than the other? Don't get me wrong, while I seek eternal rest and the chance to see my baby again; I'm not ready for it to happen at this moment.

2:32AM

I used to wonder how someone could commit suicide or what they thought before they did it.

Now I know.

Grief is hard and at your most vulnerable state, it possesses the power to consume you. This is why no one should ever offer their opinion on how you should grieve.

Grief can only be handled breath by breath because minute by minute and day by day is too long. And if you have never lost a child, don't tell a grieving mother how to handle it. Offer your hug, your smile and your condolences but keep your opinions.

My husband went to Micaela's grave, this past Monday, Memorial Day but I couldn't. Although I've pictured myself standing there, in my head, I can't physically make myself go.

The pain is still too fresh.

All I know is, this grief has to pay off in some kind of way because it hurts too badly for it all to be in vain.

Until next time.

Char.

Charlotte

"Good afternoon Charlotte, how are you today?" Dr. Mitchell ask, after I get settled on the couch.

"I'm okay."

"How have you been since our last meeting?"

"In all honesty Dr. Mitchell, I don't know how I am. One minute I think I am doing good and the next I'm crying uncontrollably."

"That is to be expected Charlotte. You suffered a major loss."

"But when does it get better?"

"I wish I had the answer. In your moments of crying, what are you feeling?"

"Sometimes I feel like I want to close my eyes and never open them again."

"As in suicide?"

I nod.

"When was the last time you had thoughts of harming yourself?"

"Last night or early this morning, the times are all running together."

"What stopped you?"

"I'm afraid to die. Even though this pain is sometimes unbearable, I am still afraid of death."

"Why is that?"

"I don't know, maybe it is fear of the unknown."

"Do you believe God has a plan for our lives?" She asks.

"I do."

"What do you believe your purpose is?"

"I haven't figured it out yet. Since losing our baby, I feel empty."

"Tell me about Micaela."

2:32AM

I sigh, trying to stop the tears that want to leap from my soul.

"She, um, she was born January fourth at 7:42pm. She was stubborn, like me, deciding she was coming on her own time." I laugh. "She had dimples, the softest hair and the sweetest smell."

"Do you have pictures of her?"

"I do but I haven't looked at them since she died."

"Why not?"

"It's too hard."

Neither of us say anything so I break the silence.

"This morning, I was on the internet and I searched for the name of mothers who have lost children."

"What did you find?"

"A lot of blogs on how to grieve and deal with the loss but nothing gives us a name."

"Do you think you need one?"

"Of course. We should be called shells."

"Why shells?"

"Because a definition of shell is an outer form without substance."

"Why do you feel you have no substance? You're alive with breath in your body, a heart and soul and in your right mind."

"Yea but what is my purpose? What kind of substance do I have? I had a baby but she died so I'm no longer a mother."

"What about being a wife?"

"A wife. Humph. Funny you should ask because I recently found out my husband is cheating with my best friend, who is pregnant. I should also mention this happened in our house on the night we buried our daughter."

"Oh Charlotte--"

"No, Dr. Mitchell, don't pity me."

2:32AM

"This isn't pity, it's an outward display of emotions. This is how you process your feelings. Try it. Tell me how you really feel, at this moment."

"I'm pissed."

"What else?"

"And I want to kill him!"

"What else?" She asks.

"I'm angry!"

"What else?"

"I feel helpless."

"What else?"

"More than anything, I feel guilty."

"Why the guilt?"

"Because I pushed him into her arms."

"You are not to blame for your husband's affair. He is a grown man who is capable of making sound decisions, the same as you. And no matter the number of times you may have pushed him away, it did not give him the right to cheat."

"He wouldn't have needed her, had I been there."

"He could have also waited Charlotte. This isn't your fault."

I wipe the tears. "I know." I say a little above a whisper. "But it still hurts."

"It's supposed too because pain lets us know we are alive and when we stop feeling anything, there is something wrong."

"What do I do?"

"You decide how you want to deal with the hurt and pain from everything you're dealing with. I want to give you something." She says getting up.

When she comes back, she hands me a journal.

"Heroin addict?" I question when I see the cover.

"Not the drug but a heroine, H-E-R-O-I-N-E, a woman who is admired for her courage." She tells me. "It's a journal intended to guide you to becoming addicted to the woman you are destined to be."

"What do you want me to do with this?"

"When you are ready, open it and start your journey to finding your substance again."

"Thank you Dr. Mitchell."

"Thank you Charlotte."

"For what?"

"For trusting the process."

When I stand, she gives me a hug.

"Would you like for me to pray with you today?"

"Not yet."

"Whenever you're ready. I'll see you Thursday."

When I make it to the car, I start the engine and lock the doors before pulling the journal from my purse. I open it and the first thing I see is the dedication page which says, *"To the woman who has to face each day pulling strength from places you didn't know existed and crying tears from areas that should have long dried up. Yet, you work a little harder, give a little more and smile while often being overlooked, overused and underpaid. This journal is dedicated to you. Thank you for never giving up, even when it seems like the easiest thing to do."*

2:32AM

Keith

"What are you reading?" I ask when I walk into the living room and see Charlotte on the couch.

"It's a journal Dr. Mitchell gave me."

"About heroin?"

"Not that it's any of your business but it's about a heroine, a woman of noble character."

"Oh, like a female hero."

"Yea."

"Is it good?"

"What do you want Keith?"

"Can we talk?"

"About what?"

"Pastor Lawson called me about your blog."

"And?"

"We are worried about you. Are you suicidal?"

"I'm suffering, not suicidal and the blog is simply a way for me to express myself. You would know had we been talking instead of you cheating."

"I messed up Charlotte and I'm sorry. I should have talked to you but you have to know I'm hurting too. You aren't the only one effected by Micaela's death."

"How would I know? You've been so distant this last month and here I was thinking it was due to the death of our baby but the whole time you've been sleeping with Dakota."

"That's not true. I am grieving our daughter."

"But why not grieve with your wife? Why did you have to turn to Dakota? Out of everything you could have turned too, why her?"

"She was here."

2:32AM

"Wow. So it was that easy?"

"Babe, none of this is easy. I made a mistake."

She throws the blanket back and gets up.

"Our daughter hadn't even been in the ground a full day and you were out back screwing my best friend. Now, she's carrying your child and I am supposed to just deal with it?"

"I'm just asking you to talk to me."

"You should have ask before you turned to her."

"I tried!"

"You should have tried harder."

"YOU WOULDN'T LET ME!"

"And that gives you the right to cheat?"

"No, but baby I messed up and I'm sorry. You wouldn't talk to me and you wouldn't let me touch you."

"It had only been six days Keith! One hundred and forty-four hours since I found our daughter cold in her crib. Eight thousand, six hundred and forty minutes since the beginning of this nightmare I cannot wake up from. If it took you six days to turn to someone else, what else will you do?"

"That's not fair. I was drinking and not in my right frame of mind."

"Neither was I but I didn't turn to some other man's penis for comfort."

"Charlotte, please give me a chance to make this right. God--"

"God? Are you seriously pulling the God card after you cheated on me? Are you seriously going to stand in my face and call God's name? God should have stopped you from cheating!"

"I'm sorry."

"We've established that."

2:32AM

"What do we do now?"

"We get divorced."

"What? No. We can work this out, please Charlotte."

"No, you being distant is what we could have worked out. You not talking to me is what we could have worked out. Us getting through this grief, is something we should have worked out but you impregnating by best friend is something we will never work out." She says walking out.

"Charlotte, I am not leaving my house!" I yell to her.

She stops and turns around.

"One of us is and it's surely not going to be me. And if you think I will allow you to stay here and have to tolerate Dakota popping up, you're crazy. Go to her apartment, I'm sure she has space for you. This way, you all can be one happy family. Maybe she can keep your child alive because I couldn't."

"Charlotte, I am not giving up on our marriage."

"You already did."

Later that night I walk into the bedroom to see Charlotte asleep. I go over, undress and climb into bed beside her.

"Hmm, Keith what are you doing?"

"Taking your clothes off."

I start to remove her pants and she doesn't stop me. I rub her thighs and I can feel her body heating up. I move in between her legs and she moans.

"Do you want me to stop?" I ask.

She shakes her head no as she pulls me closer. In a swift motion, I push her legs over my shoulders and enter her.

2:32AM

When we are done, I roll off her and pull her near me.

"Please say you'll forgive me." I say but she doesn't respond.

Charlotte

I wait until I hear Keith snoring before I slide from under his arm. I sit on the side of the bed for a minute then I grab my phone, some pajamas and underwear and walk into the guest bathroom.

I turn on the shower, remove my shirt and bra and take some towels from the closet. I hang one outside the door and step in under the hot water.

After thirty minutes or so, I get out and dry off before I get dressed. I take my phone, turn out the light in the bathroom and walk into the nursery, stopping at the door.

There are night lights around the room and the curtains were still open from the other night.

I also notice the moon is exceptionally bright.

2:32AM

We still haven't removed any of Micaela's things because it's just too hard to not have them here. And it'll make it real. I walk over to the crib and run my hand over the rail.

It's the first thing I do whenever I come into her room.

The tears were beginning to fall onto my chest. I sit in the rocking chair, open the ITunes App and press play on the song, Safe in His Arms by Avery Sunshine.

I lean my head back as I begin rocking and singing along with her.

"Because the Lord is my Shepard, I have everything I need. He lets me rests in the meadows grass and then he leads me beside the quiet stream--that's why I'm safe, that's--"

I grip the handles of the rocking chair as I feel the anger beginning to burn my throat like fire.

"Am I safe in your arms God?" I ask out loud as the tears spill from my eyes. "If I am safe, why did this have to happen to me?"

My leg begins to shake.

"My storm is raging God, do you not care? The billows are rolling God, do you not see? You said you'd hide me but where are you?"

I stand up from the chair and move over to the crib. Grabbing the blanket, I begin to scream.

"Where are you God?"

The anger, hurt and confusion begins to erupt and I start pulling everything from the crib.

"What more do you want from me?" I scream. "Why have you forsaken me? Why didn't you take me instead of her! Why God? Why?"

Screaming, I fall into the floor.

"Charlotte."

"Don't Keith, please. Just leave me alone!"

"I can't do that. Let me help you."

2:32AM

He kneels beside me.

"Baby, please let me be here for you."

I scream and begin hitting him. "Why did you let me down? You should have been here for me!"

"I'm so sorry." He cries. "I'm so sorry."

I allow him to wrap his arms around me, in the middle of the floor and we stay there until we are both done crying.

"This is what Job must have felt like, in the bible." I tell him. "It feels like I am losing everything."

"Do you remember what Job asked his wife? He asked, should we accept only good things from the hand of God and never anything bad. Charlotte, God is only testing your faith."

"He could have done it another way."

"I know but we're here now so we have to figure out a way to get through it."

I push away from him, sliding against the wall.

"I've been trying yet it seems to be getting harder."

"When was the last time you prayed?" He asks me.

"What difference does it make? God should know me."

"He does but how can He know how well your faith will sustain during times such as these, unless He allows us to go through?"

"Keith, nobody knows the strength of their faith."

"Those whose faith have been tested does. Job's faith was tested and he held on. You have to hold on to."

"To what? My husband is cheating with my best friend and my daughter is dead. What am I supposed to hold on too Keith? Huh?"

"The very thing that has not let you down, your faith in God."

"It sure feels like He has."

"By whose standards though? Death happens, we cannot stop it. Did I want our baby girl to die? No. Did I set out to break your heart? No but baby, God didn't let you down. Life did, I did but God didn't. You have to know this."

I don't say anything.

"Do you believe Charlotte?"

"I do but I am angry at God for taking her and I am angry at you for turning to somebody else."

"And that's understandable but channel your anger into overcoming, not giving up."

"I'm not giving up, I am simply having a fleshly moment." I take a breath. "Yesterday, when I left Dr. Mitchell's office, I was driving and looked in the rearview mirror and saw Micaela's seat. For a split second, I closed my eyes and remembered the few times she was back there. I've tried to take the seat out and pack up her nursery but I can't."

"It takes time." He says.

"Truth is, a part of me is afraid to get rid of her things because I feel like I'll forget her. Even though they are hard to look at, they remind me of her. It's been 52 days and I'm already forgetting the way she smelled."

"It doesn't mean you love her any less."

"It also doesn't make it easier but it's time I let these things go. You included."

"Baby–"

"Keith, please don't make this any harder. This is what I have to do for my sanity. I forgive you but I cannot be with you anymore."

2:32AM

Keith

I wake up the next morning to music playing. I roll over, already dreading the day. I get out of bed and spend the next thirty minutes showering and dressing.

I walk into the kitchen to Charlotte cooking breakfast.

"Hey you."

"Hey." She says putting biscuits in the oven.

"You seem, happy."

"This isn't happiness Keith, it's healing."

"Charlotte, I'm sorry. I know I caused you more pain with this affair but you have to know I never meant too."

"I know Keith and I'm sorry too. I had a part in pushing you into somebody else arms so will you also forgive me?"

"Of course I forgive you."

She walks over and gives me a hug.

"I have plans to clean the nursery out, this week. You are more than welcome to take anything, except the crib because I'm throwing it out. All the other stuff, I am sure will come in handy with your new baby."

"Charl–"

I am interrupted by the sound of the doorbell.

"Are you expecting anybody?" I ask her.

She shakes her head.

I go and open the door to Dakota.

"What are you doing here?" I ask through clenched teeth.

"You won't answer my calls." She says pushing her way in.

"Look, this isn't a good time."

2:32AM

"It's never a good time with you. We have to talk eventually because I am not going away."

"Why don't you join us for breakfast?" Charlotte says from behind me.

"Is this a joke?" Dakota says.

"No but you are right, we do need to talk so come into the kitchen."

Dakota and I look at each other. I close the door and she follows me into the kitchen.

"Have a seat. Would you like coffee?" Charlotte asks.

"Um, no thanks."

"Keith?"

"Sure." I say hesitating.

She sits the cup of coffee in front of me and then goes over to the stove while Dakota and I sit in silence. For over twenty minutes she finish preparing bacon, sausage, eggs, biscuits and grits.

She places everything on the table before getting glasses and orange juice.

She sits down.

"Keith, can you say grace?"

"Suurre." I say. "God, thank you for this food we are about to eat. Please remove impurities and bless the hands of the cook. Amen."

I don't immediately fix my plate.

"Dig in." Charlotte says piling food on hers.

After she takes a few bites, she looks at us.

"How far along are you?" She ask Dakota.

"Look, I don't know what is going on but this is crazy."

"No, what's crazy is my best friend being pregnant by my husband. This is me being civil."

"So, are you planning to help him raise the baby too?" Dakota asks.

"Oh no ma'am but since you showed up at my house, I thought it only right I let you know something."

"What?" Dakota questions folding her arms.

"I forgive you."

Dakota laughs. "You forgive me?"

"Yeah. See, you've been a snake since college so I knew it was only a matter of time before your scales showed. You use people, it's your nature and I knew better but I kept extending you grace. However, I don't blame you, I blame him because he's the one I took vows with."

"Then why keep me around?"

"I thought you would change but you're not my problem anymore, you're Keith's."

"Doesn't that make it yours too, seeing you're still married?" She smirks.

"Not for long. I've asked Keith for a divorce."

Dakota's eyes light up.

"Don't get any crazy ideas." I tell her. "I have no plans to marry you. Yes, I will be there for this child but I will spend every waking moment trying to win my wife back."

"Don't bother." Charlotte says spreading jelly on her biscuit. "Oh, I am cleaning out Micaela's nursery. You are welcome to anything in there except the crib."

"I don't want your hand-me-downs." She states.

"Um sweetie, that is not true because you want my husband."

"Yeah because you didn't. I was only comforting him, something you should have done."

"Oh, so not only are you an expert on cheating but you are on grief too? Well, who knew?" Charlotte says biting her bacon.

"I'm done with this conversation." She says getting up. "Keith, I have a doctor's appointment on Thursday and I expect you to be there."

"Send me the information Dakota and I will do my best."

She storms out and I turn back to look at Charlotte.

"Charlotte, is this what you really want?"

She lays her fork down.

"Keith, do you really think I want to lose my marriage right after losing my baby? Do you actually think this is what I wanted? I didn't do this, you did and if you think I am going to stand for your baby's mother consistently popping up at my house every time she feels like it, you are sadly mistaken. You made this bed boo, lay in it."

"Will you at least give me time to find somewhere to stay?"

"You have two weeks."

2:32AM | June 19, 2017

Blog Title: Funny how life changes!

It's 2:32am and once again I am up, sitting in the floor of the nursery.

Does anyone else find it funny how life changes?

Not the gut busting funny but the laugh to keep from crying kind of funny. Or the laugh to keep from killing somebody kind of funny.

It can't just be me, right?

Anyway, it's been a few weeks since I wrote you guys so I wanted to give you an update.

I asked my husband for a divorce.

I know you may think this is too big of a decision to make while grieving but trust me, it had to be made. When you find out your husband had an affair with your best friend and produced a baby, it was either a divorce or a jail cell.

I choose divorce.

Didn't I tell you life is funny? Baby, life changes when you're ready for it and even when you're not.

As for me, it has been 70 days without my sweet girl and thirteen days without my husband. I am missing them both but it's a part of life.

Isn't it?

I wake up some mornings and for a quick moment, I forget. I forget the pain of losing her until I walk pass the door of the nursery. I forget the pain of my marriage ending until I come home to an empty house.

Other days, I want to smile but then I feel guilty. Then I realize, by way of a lot of sleepless mornings, life will go on. With or without me and whether I smile or not.

Life is funny that way.

So I made it up in my mind, I will live. Through grief and divorce, I will survive.

What about you?

Oh, my therapist gave me a journal called Heroine Addict. Before you think of the drug, it's not that but HEROINE, as in a female hero.

It has been a life saver for me and there is one part I want to share with those of you who may read this post. The journal has the letters of heroine broken down into words. Without giving the entire journal away, let me share with you something the author penned for the letter N.

Notwithstanding.

"Notwithstanding what you've had to go through, you are still blessed. In spite of the obstacles placed on your path, you are still walking it. Aside from what you have had to endure, you still trust God."

2:32AM

She goes on to share this ...

"Girl, you were made for this! Girl, you got this! Girl, this is yours! I know because when God created you, He did so with the strength to persevere and overcome. All you have to do is change the way you talk. Instead of saying I can't, say notwithstanding what man says about me, I am still worthy. Instead of saying, I am broke, say notwithstanding my finances, I shall not be without. Instead of saying, the darkness will overtake me, say notwithstanding my weeping, joy will come."

Y'all, I am changing the way I talk, starting tonight (this morning).

Notwithstanding my pain, I still trust God.

I don't know why God chose me for this battle but I am here now and I can either succumb to my injuries or I can survive.

And just maybe He chose me because He knew I would survive. Not just for me but for you too.

Isn't it funny how life changes?

Until next time.

Char.

2:32AM

Charlotte

"Good afternoon Charlotte, how are you today?" Dr. Mitchell ask.

"Why do you always start by asking the same question?"

"Because knowing how you are sets the tone for our meeting."

"Oh, well I'm good." I smile.

"It has been a few weeks since I've seen you. How have you been?"

"Surviving one breath at a time."

She smiles.

"I asked Keith for a divorce."

"And how do you feel about that?"

"Um, some days it's hard especially when the house is quiet but it is for the best."

"Are you sure?"

"Very."

"What do you do to pass the time? Have you started using your journal?"

"I have but I also started a blog. I don't know if I told you the last time I was here."

"No, you didn't. What's the blog about?"

"Nothing in general but everything. If that makes sense."

"It does. Tell me, how has it helped?"

"Surprisingly, it has been another form of therapy and I've been getting a lot of responses from others who are in my shoes. Dr. Mitchell, I didn't realize the number of mothers who have gone through this."

"Has it helped you to sleep?"

"No but it is getting better."

"What about your relationship with God?"

2:32AM

"That's a work in progress but the journal has helped. Being able to write my thoughts has been a release for me. Who knows, maybe I'll take my pain and grief and write a book."

"I am glad to hear you are expressing your feelings but you need to remember you are in the midst of grief and making drastic decisions shouldn't be done during this time."

"Grief isn't the reason I have made the decision to divorce my husband, his cheating was."

"Have you thought about bringing him to one of your sessions or talking to a marriage counselor?"

"I don't need too. My mind is made up."

"Charlotte, think about this."

"He cheated with my best friend!" I say getting up from the couch. "Dr. Mitchell, look, I understand the stages of grief. Sometimes, I go through all of them before the day is over but my decision to divorce Keith is solely for my peace of mind."

"Okay, take a breath."

"I apologize for yelling but I don't need any more time to know my marriage is over. It was over the moment I found out my husband screwed my best friend, in our backyard while I cried myself to sleep, the night of our daughter's memorial. He doesn't get the chance to make it right."

"I didn't mean to make you upset. Have a seat."

We sit in silence for a few minutes.

"Charlotte, can I pray for you?"

"Not yet Dr. Mitchell but soon."

I walk into Pyro's Pizza but I don't see who I am looking for so I get in line to place my order.

2:32AM

"Good evening, what's the name on your pizza?"

"Charlotte."

"Would you like to add a drink or maybe dessert?"

"I'll take a drink and the sweet bites. Why not, you only live once, right?"

She laughs. "Do you have a reward card?"

"No."

"Okay, your total is $13.47."

I go to hand the young lady my card but someone calls my name. I turn and look into the face of a nice looking gentleman.

"Hi, I'm Conner. Please let me buy your dinner tonight since I am the reason you're here." He says handing the young lady his card.

"You didn't have to do that."

The young lady hands him his card, receipt and buzzer for my pizza.

"It is my pleasure."

I smile. "Why don't I find us a table while you get your food?"

"Will do."

After a few minutes, he comes over to the table. I am replying to a comment on the blog so I don't immediately look up.

When I do he is smiling at me.

"My apology for being rude." I tell him.

"Oh it's no problem."

"Do you normally handle all your business transactions over dinner?" I ask him.

"No and I'm sorry. If you are uncomfortable, we can reschedule and you can come to my office."

"No, no; I didn't mean to insinuate that I was uncomfortable, it was just a question."

He takes a sip of his drink.

2:32AM

"Usually, I would have come to you but since we've had a hard time catching each other, I decided to try dinner."

A young man sits my pizza in front of me. I bow my head and say grace. Before I can say anything, his pizza is bought out and he does the same thing.

"Now tell me a little about what you're needing."

"My daughter passed away, a few months back and I want to do something to remember her."

"I am so sorry to hear that."

"Thank you."

"How old was she?"

"Three months."

"Man, that's a hard one."

"It definitely has been hard."

"Do you have anything specific in mind for the memorial?"

I reach into my purse and pull out a picture.

"I found this online. It doesn't have to be exactly like this but I would like a sitting area with maybe a bench or swing."

"Do you mind if I keep this?"

"Sure. Have you ever done anything like this before?"

"Yes."

"I'm sorry because that was a crazy question. What I meant was, have you ever done a backyard memorial like this for a baby? I went on your website and it didn't show any."

"I understood what you meant and to answer your question, we have done a few of these. Usually we create headstones but we have been able to design a memorial like the one you have in mind."

2:32AM

"How long have you been in business?"

"My father and I have been creating memorials such as this for over ten years now. We started after my mom passed away."

"We haven't been separated a month and you're already seeing somebody?"

I look up at Keith.

"Keith, what are you doing?"

"Me? What are you doing?"

"I'm having dinner and you are causing a scene. Go home--" I stop when I see Dakota walking towards him. "Or rather, go and have dinner with your baby's mother."

She grabs him by the arm and he gives me a scowling look before leaving.

"I am so sorry."

"An ex?"

"Almost."

Conner laughs.

We spend the next hour talking and going over details of what I want him to create in the backyard before I make an appointment for him to come and take measurements in a few days.

2:32AM | July 4, 2017

Blog Title: Independence Day

It's 2:32am and I'm up. Yes, I am sitting in the middle of the nursery. I wish I could tell you I've finally cleaned it out but I haven't. Crazy thing is, it seems to be my place of solitude.

I can come in here and sit for hours, usually with music playing. It also helps because my sleep schedule is off and without an alarm, I find myself waking up around 2:30.

Almost every day.

It has gotten easier because it was every night.

I don't know how this is going to work when I am supposed to go back to work next week. The blessing, I work for my father's law firm so he's a little of a pushover. (Don't tell him I said it. LOL)

For all of my working moms, how do you deal with the sad looks and questions once you're back in society? Sure, I've been to the grocery store and to get food but those people don't know my daughter died 85 days ago.

Going back to work is facing those who threw me a baby shower. I mean, I left there pregnant and now I'm going back as a shell of a person without a baby.

Ugh!

Anyway, Happy Fourth of July everyone. I hope this Independence Day is great for each of you. If you get a chance, say a prayer for me because I'm not feeling my best. I'm going to try and get some sleep before my parents show up to drag me to some backyard barbecue.

Until next time.

Char.

2:32AM

Keith

"Good morning, can I help you?"

"Yes, my baby's mother has an appointment today and I was trying to see if she's already gone to the back?"

"Her name?"

"Dakota Marshall."

"One moment."

"Are you sure it's today?"

"Yes, today is the sixth of July, right?"

"Yes sir but she doesn't have an appointment."

"Her name is D-A-K-O-T-A Marshall."

"Sir, I can spell her name but she does not have an appointment today."

"Thank you."

I grab my phone and turn to call Dakota when I bump into… "Charlotte?"

"Keith, what are you doing here?"

"I was supposed to meet Dakota for a doctor's appointment but I must have gotten the days mixed up. What are you doing here?"

"For an appointment."

"Are you pregnant?"

She looks away.

"Charlotte, are you pregnant?"

"I don't know yet."

"Mrs. Hulbert, we have a room for you now." The nurse calls out.

"I'll call you."

When she walks off, I stand there for a minute until my phone vibrates.

2:32AM

"Dakota, where are you? What? No, I'm here at the doctor's office. I can't hear you, speak up. I'm on the way."

"Ms. Parrish, you're in pain because you have appendicitis. We will need to perform surgery in order to remove it."

I hear the doctor tell Dakota when I walk into the hospital room.

"We will do a laparoscopic procedure, where we will place three small incisions in your abdomen. If we are unable to remove the appendix through this method, we will place a larger incision--"

"Wait," I say interrupting. "What about the baby?"

"Baby?" The doctor questions. "What baby?"

"She's pregnant."

The doctor looks from me to Dakota.

"I'm not." She says.

"What?"

"I'm not pregnant Keith."

"What do you mean?" I yell.

"Sir, you will need to calm down."

"Calm down? Have you been lying this entire time?"

"I wasn't lying. I had a miscarriage."

"When?"

"A few days after you moved out from Charlotte."

"This is un-freaking-believable."

"I'm sorry Keith but I need you. Please don't leave me."

2:32AM

"Sir, I don't know what's going on but we're about to take her into surgery and I need her to calm down."

"Keith, I promise I will explain everything but please don't leave. I don't want to be alone when I wake up. Please."

"Oh, I'll be here when you wake up. Trust me."

A few hours later, Dakota is bought into the room. She is still groggy from the anesthesia so I wait.

"Keith."

I open my eyes to see Dakota awake.

"I'm so sorry." She cries.

"Are you okay?"

She nods her head.

"Dakota, why wouldn't you tell me you lost the baby?"

"I didn't want to lose you."

"This was not the way to handle things. You know Charlotte is going through a tough time right now--"

"It's not about Charlotte. I love you and if you give us a chance I know we can make this work."

"This isn't love Dakota, it is lust and infatuation. We had sex, one night, when I wasn't thinking clearly. You don't get love from that."

"Please Keith. I know I messed up but we can try again."

"You are not in the right frame of mind to even have this conversation, at the moment. We will talk but I have to go."

"Don't leave me. Keith! Please!"

She is screaming so loud, when I open the door, it causes a nurse to run in.

"KEITH!"

2:32AM

I drive over to our home, barely letting the car stop before I jump out, running to the door.

I keep ringing the doorbell until Charlotte opens it.

"Keith, what's wrong?"

"I need to talk to you."

"Are you okay? Why are you ringing the doorbell like the house is on fire?"

"This cannot wait, I need to talk to you now."

Just then a dude walks in the back door without a shirt on.

"Who is this?" I ask pushing pass her. "Is that the dude you were having dinner with?

"Excuse you? You lost the privilege to question anything I do."

"You're still my wife!"

"Not for long. Now, what do you want because it's obvious I am in the middle of something?"

"Mrs. Charlotte, I don't mean to interrupt but I need you. It'll only take a minute."

"He needs you?"

"Wait here." She says to me before turning to follow dude outside.

I go right behind her.

"What's wrong?"

"The bench is a little bigger than we expected so I will need to cut into the flowers you have back here. I can extend it out, this way," he says pointing. "Is that okay?"

"Yes, you–"

"Hold on, you don't have permission to tear up my yard. Who are you?"

"Keith, you need to calm down."

2:32AM

"You have another man, in my house making changes to what I've worked hard for and you're telling me to calm down."

Just then, the rest of Conner's crew walks through the back yard.

"As if I need to explain anything to you but this is Conner and he is creating a memorial for our daughter. This way I will not have to think about my husband having sex with another woman every time I walk back here. Now, get out of my house."

My mouth drops.

"Conner, you have my permission to do whatever you need to make this memorial garden. If it means restructuring the entire yard, do it because it holds nothing but bad memories."

"Yes ma'am."

I follow her into the house.

"Charlotte, wait."

"What Keith? What else would you like to accuse me of? Unlike you, I don't sleep with random people."

"I'm sorry."

"You've become good at apologizing. Just say what you came here to say and leave."

"Dakota is not pregnant."

"Congratulations."

"Did you hear what I said? She is not pregnant anymore."

"What do you want? An award or a happy for you? Sorry boo but I have nothing."

"Baby--Charlotte, I want to come home. You said--"

"I know what I said Keith."

"There is no baby, she had a miscarriage a few weeks ago."

2:32AM

"And that's supposed to make everything right with us again? You still cheated on me, with my best friend."

"I know and I will spend the rest of my life making it up to you. Please, just give me another chance. I love you Charlotte and I do not want to live without you."

"Did you have anything to do with her losing the baby?"

"No! Why would you ask me something like that?"

She shrugs.

"Baby please. I know I messed up by sleeping with Dakota but can't we go to counseling or something?"

"Keith, I appreciate your apology and I am sorry Dakota lost the baby but I am finally getting used to being by myself. I am dealing with the grief of our daughter and I believe I can finally see some light at the end of the tunnel so my answer is no. I am still moving forward with the divorce."

"All I am asking is for you to please think about it."

I walk over to the door but I stop.

"Wait, what did the doctor say? Are you pregnant?"

"No." She says. "And next time, call before you drop by."

2:32AM

Charlotte

I watch Keith leave before walking to the back door to watch Conner and his men work.

"Push baby!"

"Oh God, this hurts!"

"I know but she's almost here."

"Charlotte, take a deep breath and give me one more push." Dr. Meade says.

"I can't. I'm tired, just cut me or something because I can't."

"You got this babe, it's just one more push!"

"Shut up Keith!"

"Charlotte, you're going to have to calm down. Take a breath and bear down when I tell you too." The doctor says. "Okay, push!"

Wailing is heard throughout the room.

"She's here Charlotte, our baby girl is here!"

"Would you like to cut the cord?" The nurse asks Keith holding out the scissors.

"Heck yeah!" He sings.

The nurse whisk the baby off to the waiting incubator.

"What's wrong with her?"

"Nothing, were just getting her cleaned up and checking her vitals."

The baby is still crying and the more she does, the more Keith does until he grabs her hand and begins to sing a slow rendition of Happy Birthday in her ear which quiets her down.

"She knows daddy's voice." The nurse says continuing to work.

"Is she ok? How much does she weigh?"

"She's six pounds, six ounces and 21 inches long." The nurse answers.

2:32AM

After cleaning her up, making impressions of her feet and all the other newborn stuff, she's wrapped up and placed in Keith's arms.

"What are we naming her?"

"I thought we agreed on Micaela Olivia Hulbert."

"Yea but I also know you've changed your mind one hundred times."

"No, it's final. Her name is Micaela Olivia Hulbert."

"Thank you God."

Tapping on the door causes me to jump, bringing me out of my thoughts.

"Ms. Charlotte, we have to let the concrete set before we place the bench and the other pieces. We will be back, first thing in the morning to finish."

"Thank you Conner. I will leave about 7:30 but if there is anything you need, please don't hesitate to call me."

"Yes ma'am."

When they leave, I lock up the house and turn the alarm on. I fix me a quick, microwave meal for dinner and once I am done, I head for the bedroom.

Tomorrow is my first day back at work and I don't have a clue what I am going to wear. For the last few months, all I have had to decide between was sweats or jeans.

I open the closet and see most of Keith's clothes still hanging there. I run my hand across his suits, ties, tees and jeans. I pull one of his shirts off the hanger to smell it.

Then I break down into tears.

"Why couldn't I be enough for him? Why did he have to turn to her?"

2:32AM

I fall onto my knees in the floor and for the first time, I call God's name out of desperation instead of anger.

"God, show me your face because I am tired of pushing you away, tired of fighting you and so very tired of being angry. Please show me what you will have me to do. If my marriage is worth saving, give me a sign because God, I can no longer do this on my own. I know you taking Micaela was part of your plan, forgive me for ever questioning your will. I know things happen that are not in my control, forgive me for ever thinking I could do it myself. I need you God. I need you for my strength and peace of mind. God, I'm sorry."

I move and the stiffness of my body lets me know I've fallen asleep in the closet. I look around and I am still holding Keith's shirt.

I slowly get up and stretch.

I still need to pick something out for tomorrow but it'll have to wait.

2:32 AM | July 11, 2017

Blog Title: To work again ...

Another morning and I am up.

AGAIN!

No, I am not sitting in the floor of the nursery but does that really make a difference, especially when I have to be at work in a few hours?

My body keeps waking me up with an internal alarm, set for this time.

What is God trying to tell me? Anyone know? Maybe I should ask Him but before tonight I hadn't prayed to God in months. Yes, I've yelled and screamed at Him but praying. NOPE.

I was losing faith in God.

Then I realized, my anger is only hindering me. It is stopping me from seeing the potential purpose in everything that has happened. And I don't know about any of you, who have experienced grief, but I definitely need to see the reason for this type of pain.

Could it be to help others? Could it be to bring me and my husband closer? Could it be preparing me for something greater?

Maybe I will talk to my pastor about it.

Oh, my husband stopped by yesterday to ask for another chance but I don't know. I told him I would think about it and I will, however he crossed a very thin line.

But tonight, I prayed for God to give me a sign and when He does, I'll take it. Good (if He tells me to repair the marriage) or bad (continue with the divorce).

Anyway, I am rambling which happens when you are tired.

On another note, I do have some good news to share. I am having a memorial built in the

2:32AM

backyard. It's nothing fancy, just an area for me to sit, think and write.

The construction company I found is amazing. Conner, the owner, designed a bench with Micaela's name, her date of birth and death and even her footprints. It's so cool. I will have to post pictures once it's done.

It's been 92 days. *Sigh.*

Until next time.

Char.

Charlotte

I roll over, cringing before silencing the alarm. After my shower and other morning duties, I get dressed in the usual business attire.

I chose a pencil skirt with a blouse, jacket and pumps. Standing in front of the mirror, my stomach is in knots.

"You got this girl!" I repeat a couple of times.

I grab my phone and walking out the room, I stop at the door of the nursery.

"Momma is taking it a breath at a time sweet pea."

I grab my computer bag and purse and head for the car.

Finally, pulling into the parking lot I turn off the engine, close my eyes and take a few deep breaths.

2:32AM

Walking into the building, I feel like a new employee.

"Welcome back Mrs. Charlotte." David, head of security says. "Here is your new badge. The old one expired while you were gone."

"Thank you David. I hope you were able to keep my dad under control."

"I did the best I could ma'am." He laughs. "It is good to have you back."

"Thank you and it is good to be back."

When I get off the elevator, I am met with balloons and all the staff.

"Welcome back Charlotte!" They all scream.

I stand there for a few seconds before I burst into tears.

"Oh, we are so sorry. We didn't mean to make you cry." Janice says handing me a tissue and taking my bags.

"Thank you guys." I say while wiping my face. "I have received all of your cards, flowers and I have felt your prayers. It feels good to know you all loved Micaela just as much as I did. All I ask is for you bear with me. There may be more moments with tears and if you happen to see me, during those times, all I need is a hug. Thank you all again."

After the hugging, I finally reach my desk. I don't even get to sit down before there is a tap on the door.

"Hey, don't get too comfortable, I need your help."

"Ah dad, I haven't even had coffee."

"Grab it on your way to my office."

"I'll get it later. What's so urgent?" I ask walking to catch up with him.

"This." He says pointing to the table in his office.

2:32AM

"What are--" I gasp when I pick up one of the pictures. "Are you all hell bent on making this an emotional day?"

"I'm sorry baby girl, I didn't mean to make you cry again."

"Dad, I, um I forgot we had these taken."

He walks over to me and I bury my head in his shoulder. He leads me over to the couch, handing me a handkerchief from his pocket.

"I haven't looked at a picture of her since she's been gone. Why do you have these out?"

"I was having them framed, for you, but an executive from Healthy Baby saw them on yesterday and wants to include them in their new ad campaign."

"What? No. Did you explain to them she's um—that she's--"

"I did but listen to me." He says grabbing my arm. "Calm down and listen. Their current marketing campaign is to educate parents on SIDS."

"Oh dad."

"Charlotte, think about everything you've gone through. This is a great opportunity to share the pain and sleepless nights SIDS left you with. And as a warning for other parents."

"Nobody warned me?"

"Shouldn't this be more of a reason for us to partner with them on this?"

"Dad, SIDS is Sudden Infant Death Syndrome. There is no cure and no 100% effective method to prevent it. I know because we tried. I am all for them doing their PSAs and commercials but I don't know about them using Micaela's pictures. It's too hard."

He doesn't say anything.

"What else aren't you telling me?"

"They also want to interview you."

"Dang it dad. Could you not have warn me about this before today?"

"I could have but we both know you probably wouldn't have shown up."

"You're probably right." I laugh. "Let me think on it. When do you have to give them an answer?"

"By Monday."

"I will talk to Keith and let you know."

I spent the rest of the afternoon getting caught up. My email is full of condolences from clients and I have had to field the overload of welcome back calls.

Don't get me wrong, I am appreciative of people for taking their time to offer words of comfort but it can be draining.

I leave the office, a little after five, stopping to pick up some takeout for dinner. Getting home, I decide to take my shower first before eating.

Afterwards, I get the takeout container, a fork and bottle of water and head into the bedroom. Sitting in the middle of the bed, I open my computer and log into my social media account.

I haven't been on any form of social media since Micaela's death because I didn't have the energy to respond to all of the 'sorry for your loss,' 'you have my deepest condolences' and 'praying for' comments.

When my page loads, the first thing that pops up is a picture of Dakota and Keith.

"Wow." I say laughing. I click on Dakota's name and see she's changed her status to 'In a Relationship.'

I scroll through the 212 comments. Some of them are congratulatory while the rest are from people who know the both of us.

2:32AM

They, just like me, are angry to find out about them. I politely unfriend and block Dakota because Keith is not on Facebook.

I grab my phone and dial his number.

"Charlotte, hey."

"Hey Keith, we need to talk."

"Sure, when?"

"Now, can you stop by?"

"I can be there in fifteen."

"Use your key."

I take my food and phone and walk back into the living room to eat while waiting for Keith.

"Hey you." He says.

"Hey."

"Man your food smells good."

"You are welcome to have some."

"You sure? I don't want to intrude on your dinner."

"Boy, I can hear your stomach growling over here." I say handing him the container and fork.

I give him a few minutes to eat.

"Can I ask you a question?"

"Yea," he says with his mouth full.

"Are you still sleeping with Dakota?"

He swallows. I hand him my water bottle and wait for him to finish.

"Babe, I promise with everything in me, no. I was only with her the one time."

"I saw her Facebook page and she has a picture of the two of you saying you're in a relationship."

"That's a lie. The last time I saw her was when she tried to explain away the fact she'd been lying."

2:32AM

"What happened?"

He sits the food down.

"Apparently, she had a miscarriage the day after I moved out but never said anything. The more I think about it, she probably never would have, had it not been for her appendix rupturing."

"I am not shocked."

"Charlotte, I am so sorry for ever causing you this kind of pain. It was never my intention but I am willing to do whatever it takes to get you to love me again."

"Keith, I do love you but my trust in you is shaky."

"I understand but please say you believe me."

I sigh. "I do and I am willing to try and fix this between us. It doesn't mean you can move back in but I want you to come with me to my next counseling session. I have an appointment with Dr. Mitchell Thursday at 1."

"I'll be there."

"There's something else. Two things actually. One of dad's accounts wants to interview me about Micaela's death. They also want to use some of her pictures in a PSA on SIDS."

"How do you feel about that?"

"At first I said no but if it'll help somebody else, it may be a good idea."

"I will support you either way."

"Thanks."

"What's the other thing?"

"I lied to you and I am sorry."

"About what?"

"I am pregnant."

2:32AM

Keith

When I get to the car, I replay Charlotte's words over and over in my head.

"I am pregnant."

I begin to laugh out loud but then the sound changes to crying.

"Oh God, I am so sorry. Forgive me for not being a better husband. Forgive me for allowing the weakness of my flesh to overshadow my vows. I know I should have been there for my wife but I wasn't. I promise, if you let us make it through this, I will rededicate my life back to you and her. Reconnect us, oh God. Amen."

I sit there a few more minutes before calling my pastor. The phone connects to the Bluetooth.

"Deacon Hulbert, how are you this evening."

"Pastor, I really need to talk to you."

"Of course son, come to the house."

"Yes sir."

"I'll be waiting for you."

I make the twenty minute drive to the Lawson Residence. Walking up to the door, Pastor Lawson opens it.

"Keith, are you okay?"

"I really messed up Pastor and I don't know how to fix it."

"When we don't know, God does. Come on in."

He leads me to his study.

"Can I get you anything to drink?"

"No sir."

"Have a seat and tell me what's going on?"

"I cheated on my wife."

"I know."

I look at him.

"Charlotte wrote it on her blog."

"I really messed up."

"Son, we all make mistakes but what are you going to do to fix it?"

"Whatever it takes."

"Now, before you make this broad statement you need to realize the power of your words. Saying whatever it takes means just that and it may include some things you don't like."

"Pastor, I cannot lose my wife. We've been through too much as it is."

"Then why did you cheat?"

"A lapse in judgment."

"What is Charlotte saying?"

"Initially she asked for a divorce but tonight she said she's willing to give me another chance."

"What about the young lady you had the affair with? Isn't she pregnant?"

"No sir, not anymore. She lost the baby a few weeks ago."

"Have you made it clear to her your intentions?"

"Yes sir. I made them perfectly clear in the beginning. She knew there was no relationship between us, I was strictly being there for the baby."

"Keith, yes you messed up but you can be forgiven. When Peter asked Jesus how many times should I only forgive someone who sins against me seven times? Jesus replied in Matthew eighteen and verse twenty-two; no, not seven times but seventy times seven. What I am sharing with you is, no man is perfect who walks this earth. Ask your wife for forgiveness. Now, while she has a responsibility to give it, it is at her time."

"Yes sir."

"Also hear me when I tell you this. Just because Charlotte gives you forgiveness, it doesn't make all of your problems go away. You hurt your wife, son, during a time when the two of you should have been healing together. You hurt her at a time when she needed you the most so there will be days and nights, in the midst of the repair, her anger gets the best of her. Let her get through it. The times when she pushes you away, stand there and let her. The times when she may turn her back to you, be there when she turns again. In other words, give her time. Remember you said, you'll be willing to do whatever it takes."

"I did and I mean it."

"Then be ready to pray more because the enemy will show up with a vengeance to try and tear down what God has joined together. As the man, you have to be even stronger now because the spirit is telling me your storm isn't over yet. And this time, it's going to take the two of you to make it through. Are you willing?"

"Yes sir, I am. I am willing and I mean this, to do whatever it takes to save my wife. Grief almost cost me everything and I cannot allow it to win. It cannot win Pastor. It can't." I say breaking down.

"Let me cover you son." He says walking over and putting his hand on my back.

"God in heaven who is the giver and taker of life, sustainer and repairer of our mind, redeemer, way maker, heart fixer and mind regulator. God, I come tonight bombarding heaven on behalf of Keith and Charlotte Hulbert. Lord, I don't have to list their needs, you already know them. I don't have to give you a rundown of their misdeeds, you know them too. All I am asking for tonight, master, is for your strength to deliver. God, through my hands, release the power to resist the enemy. God, through my words, unleash the anointing of the Holy Ghost to intercede for this family. I know their storm isn't over so I need you to surround them with people and the things they need to survive

2:32AM

this. God, you said all I had to do was ask, so I'm asking for you to do it. Make a way we cannot see. Send Keith home to retake his rightful place. God, stay the hand of the enemy so nothing he tries will succeed. It is so, by the blood of our crucified savior. Amen."

Charlotte

I groan as I turn over in the bed. I've been laying here for hours trying to sleep. I touch the home button on my phone and see a new comment added to the blog.

I sit up and open it.

"Hey! You don't know me but I recently found your blog while searching the internet and I wanted to say thank you! Your posts have helped me when it feels like I am about to lose my mind. My son died, seven months ago from SIDS and no matter what I do, I cannot get the image of him out of my head. How are you so strong? Please help me."

I lay the phone down and close my eyes trying to figure out how can I possibly help somebody when I'm still walking on an unsteady bridge of emotions.

"Strong? Me?" I say out loud.

"Lord, what can I say to another mother who is in the midst of grief?"

Then I remember the scripture hanging in the nursery. I throw the covers back and run across the hall.

Turning on the light, I go over to the wall and read the plaque I'd hung there when we'd first started decorating the nursery.

"Blessed is she who has believed that the Lord would fulfill his promises to her! – Luke 1:45"

Okay God.

I turn off the light and go back to my room. I pick the phone back up.

"Hey, thank you for reaching out to me. I know, all too well, the feeling of being helpless. It is one I would not grant to my worst enemy. I wish I had the magic answer to help you but the truth is, I don't. Thank you for thinking of me as being strong because I am anything but. There are days I close my eyes and I can still hear her cry but I know she's gone. Then there are days, it feels like her memories are slipping away and no matter what I do, I cannot make them stay. Both days are hard but we have to keep going.

Your days AND nights will get easier. I don't know when but I believe they will. And take consolation in knowing your son and my daughter are resting in an eternal rest and we will see them again. As you said, you don't know me but I hope you will do something for me. Stop being angry at God. I know it's hard, in fact, I only recently stopped myself but if I have learned anything, it is we need Him.

Through our good and bad days, we need Him. Know He did not intentionally cause you this unbearable pain because He didn't have anything else to do but this pain is a somber reminder we are alive with a purpose we must fulfill. I will be praying for you my sister. "

2:32AM

I lay the phone down. As much as I want to blog tonight, sleep was calling and I gratefully answer.

Therapy Session with Keith

"Good afternoon Charlotte, how are you?"

"I am good Dr. Mitchell, how are you?"

"I am good. Is your husband going to join us?"

"He is but I asked him to give us a few minutes."

"Okay, what's going on?"

"Am I making the right decision?"

"What do you mean, by inviting him here?"

"No, by giving him another chance. Dr. Mitchell, he slept with my best friend."

"Charlotte, he made a mistake. Yes, it was a big one but it is still a mistake. I cannot tell you what to do but I can offer my advice and my advice is, be willing to offer him grace as God does us."

2:32AM

"I'm trying but it is hard. It was so easy for him to cheat before, what's to keep him from doing it again?"

"What makes you think it was easy for him? Have you asked him?"

"No."

"Then you cannot just assume it was. Let me bring in your husband. It's only fair we give him a chance to speak for himself."

"Joya, please send Mr. Hulbert in."

I open the door.

"Mr. Hulbert, it's nice to meet you. I'm Dr. Mitchell."

"It's nice to meet you, as well."

"Please have a seat. Charlotte, ask Keith your question."

I exhale and turn to him. "Why was it so easy for you to cheat?"

"To be honest, I don't know the answer but you have to believe I never set out to sleep with Dakota. One minute we were drinking and cleaning up and the next we were outside having sex."

"But why not tell me? Do you know how humiliating it was to have her gloat in my face about sleeping with my husband?"

"Baby, you were in so much pain and all you were doing was either sleeping or sitting in the nursery. I couldn't bring myself to break you more than you already were. I am sorry for putting you in the position to be embarrassed."

"Would you have ever told me had she not been pregnant?"

"Yes because it was weighing heavily on me."

"Charlotte, do you forgive Keith?" Dr. Mitchell interjects.

"I want too."

"What's stopping you?"

"What's to say the next time something bad happens, he doesn't repeat his same bad habit."

"Ask him."

"I won't." Keith says before I can repeat the question. "Charlotte, I am not promising to be perfect but I will never, ever cheat on you again."

"What's going to stop you though?"

"You."

"Keith, how am I going to stop you from cheating when I didn't before?"

"By giving me another chance, you are saying you believe in me. Charlotte, that's all I need."

"You say that now." I say.

"Charlotte, remember grace. Grace is God giving us what we don't deserve. No matter how many times we mess up, God is still right there extending us grace. With this being said Keith, you have to know your responsibility as a husband is far more than simply being the head of your household.

The bible tells us in Ecclesiastes nine, verse nine, to enjoy life with the woman whom you love all the days of your fleeting life which He has given to you under the sun; for this is your reward in life and in your toil in which you have labored under the sun."

"Thank you Dr. Mitchell."

"Don't thank me yet because I am not done. I need you to look at each other."

Keith extends his hand to me and I hesitate, at first but finally take it.

"Getting back on the road will not be easy but as long as you put your hand on the wheel, the car in gear and press the gas you can make it. Charlotte, just because Keith messed up, it doesn't give you the right to continually throw it in his face. Keith, just because you messed up, it doesn't mean you'll have to spend the rest of your life making up for it.

Taking vows, with each other, is more than reciting words spoken. Vows are a promise of commitment to love one another in sickness and in health, in poverty and in wealth, in the good that may lighten your ways and especially when bad may darken your days. Is this something you both are willing to do?"

"I am willing." He says looking at me in the eyes.

"I am too." I respond with tears falling.

"Charlotte, I apologize to you and I promise-"

"No Keith, don't promise just show me. But I want you to know we will need more than just this one session because my trust is still shaky yet I am willing to try."

"Does this mean I can come home?"

"Yes but in the guest room."

"Char–"

"Dr. Mitchell, it is a process. I am willing to forgive my husband but he has to earn his spot back in the bed."

Dr. Mitchell throws her hands up in surrender.

"I'll take it. As long as I'm under the same roof, I'll sleep in the laundry room if I have too." He says causing us to laugh.

"Then we are on the right track. Keith, how about you join us next Thursday, as well. We will keep Mondays strictly for Charlotte. Is that okay with you?"

"It is. I will be here for as long as it takes."

"What about you Charlotte? Are you alright with this change?"

"I am."

"Great. Then I look forward to seeing you again. Can I pray for the two of you before you leave?"

"It's okay with me."

"Charlotte."

"Yes, Dr. Mitchell. I am ready for prayer now."

She smiles before laying her pad and pen down. She gets up and walks over to us and we all grab hands.

"Our Father in Heaven, I come before you with a spirit of thanksgiving. Thank you God for your daughter Charlotte and your son Keith. God, only you know everything they have had to deal with so I ask you now to bless them, individually and collectively. Rain down your power of strength for them to survive. Heal Charlotte's heart and restore into her your joy.

Give peace that surpasses her understanding and don't allow her to be led astray.

For Keith, give him wisdom and understanding to be the man you have called him to be. For God, they are yours and although we may not understand why we have to suffer, we know you will never put more on us than we can handle. Thank you Father for your unyielding grace. We love you Lord and we seal this prayer with amen."

2:32AM

Keith

Walking out of the office, I pull Charlotte into a hug.

"I've missed you." She says.

"Baby, I've missed you more."

When I release her, she allows me to grab her hand while we walk to our cars.

"Are you headed back to work?" I ask her.

"No, I'm going home. You?"

"I was hoping to follow you there."

"Don't you have to get your things from wherever you've been staying?"

"Nope. I checked out of the extended stay this morning."

"Oh, so you just knew I'd let you come home?"

"No but I was praying you would." I smile.

We make it to the house and after I am done bringing my things in, I ask Charlotte if she'd like to go out to eat and she agreed.

We decide on Pizza.

Opening her door, I take her hand to help her out the car.

"Have you tried this place before?"

"No but I heard it was good from a few of my co-workers."

"Good evening, how many in your party?"

"Two."

"Right this way."

The hostess seats us at a table.

"Have either of you ever been to Rock N Dough?" She ask once we're seated.

"No, it's our first time."

"You will see from the menu we have an array of things to choose from. Of course, our specialty is pizza but everything else is great as well. Your server for tonight will be Chaka."

"Deacon Hulbert."

"Pastor Lawson, how are you sir?" I ask standing to shake his hand.

"I am great. How are you?"

"I am great as well."

"Charlotte, it is so good to finally lay eyes on you."

"Pastor Lawson, it feels great to be seen." She says standing to give him a hug.

"How have you been?"

"I've been making it."

"Well you know we miss you at church and we cannot wait to hear your beautiful voice of again."

"Thank you Pastor. I have plans to be there on Sunday. I don't know if I'm ready to sing yet but we will see."

"Your microphone will be waiting when you are. I'm going to let you all get back to dinner. It was great seeing the two of you."

"Pastor Lawson, please give Lady Lawson my love."

"I will. Enjoy your night."

Charlotte and I spend the rest of the night enjoying each other's company. I can't remember the last time we've had this chance and I don't take it for granted.

2:32 AM | August 3, 2017

Blog Title: Another Chance

Its 2:32 and I am up. In my defense, I got up to use the restroom and couldn't go back to sleep. I know it has been almost a month since I last blogged so I decided to give you all an update.

115 days.

This is how long it has been without our sweet girl. Yes, days are still hard and nights are harder but I am still here. The memorial in the back yard is finally done and I have decided to have a small unveiling for our family.

It is beautiful.

And I cried.

A lot.

Good thing, Keith has been here for me. I decided to let him move back home. He's sleeping in the guest room but we are finding our way back to each other.

Is this too much information to share?

Shrugs.

Anyway, I have forgiven him by the same measure of grace God forgives me.

Another chance, right?

As for my ex-best friend, I have forgiven her too but we will NEVER be friends again.

Sure, you can say it is a double standard but Keith was/is willing to make amends, the ex-friend, isn't.

But whatever!

I am going back to church Sunday. I've missed the fellowship and the worship but most of all, I have missed singing.

I can remember how Micaela would look at me every time I would sing to her. It was like she could understand every word. I would always use

2:32AM

her to practice a new song and if she frowned, it means she didn't like it. LOL.

I miss her.

Oh, now I'm about to cry again which means it is time for me to sign off.

Until next time,

Char.

Charlotte

"Good morning Temple of Praise! How are you feeling this morning?"

Keith and I walk into the sanctuary, as worship begins. I almost talked myself out of coming but I need to be here.

"Will you all stand and join us in worship?" Our worship leader Angela says as the music begins. "Can you just lift your hands and worship God in this place? Has He been good to anybody? Has He kept anybody? Has He made a way for anybody? Just worship Him. That's it, worship Him because He deserves it."

I put my purse and bible in the seat. When she begins to sing, the words cause me to stop.

"You tried your way, it didn't work. You put Him second and put you first. You trusted friends, thought they had your back and every time you turn around it seems you're under

attack. But turn to your neighbor and say; the devil is a liar. No, I'm not gone die but it's okay to cry."

My hands are lifted as the tears stream down my face. Angela continues to sing and the more she does, the more it feels as if my spirit is being opened and laid before God. I want to fight and stop whatever it is that's happening to me but I can't.

I feel like no one is in the sanctuary but me as I extend my hands toward heaven and worship.

Angela sings:

"I did everything I could to take away my trouble and everything I tried did not stop my struggle. Just doing me every day, guess I was in my own way. But I'm here to tell you, without His grace I'm a major failure so if you got problems, know that you can't fix it, just give it to Jesus, oh can I get a witness."

"Who am I talking to in this place? Who is this for today? Let it out because God is trying to tell you something."

Before I can stop myself, I begin to speak in Heavenly language, in tongue as the Holy Spirit starts to intercede for me.

I cry out.

Then, Keith begins to praise. He begins to dance and for the first time, I join in.

I don't remember much after that.

By the time we are finally able to get back to our seats, I have a feeling I cannot put into words. Keith puts his hand on my back as I bend over in complete and unexplainable worship.

"Thank you Father. Thank you God. I surrender to your will. I surrender to your way. Oh God, I trust you."

Once service is over, I take a few minutes to mingle with the pastor and members before walking up front to Angela.

"Charlotte, oh my God, I am so happy to see you."

"It feels great to be seen. How are you?"

"Girl, I am blessed but more importantly, how are you?" She asks.

"Better now since I've been here."

"Amen to that."

"You've got to tell me the name of the song from earlier."

"It's called Listen by Marvin Sapp. Isn't it amazing?"

"It definitely is. Just what I needed to hear this morning."

She pulls me into a hug.

"Your nights of crying may not be over but you haven't lost your song. The enemy wants you to believe that but he is a liar. You spend as many hours as you need, sitting and singing in the dark and when you are ready, your microphone is waiting." She steps back but doesn't release my arm. "When the time comes, all you have to do is open your mouth and your song will still be there."

I look at her.

"I knew better than to come to someone prophetic." I laugh.

"You know it." She says laughing too. "Seriously Charlotte, I've been warring for you, in the spirit and God has your back. And He's not upset at you for pushing Him away but get back to Him because your days of darkness are not over and that man standing over there," she says pointing to Keith, "he's going to need you this time."

I have a confused look on my face.

"You may not understand it now but you will. Stop fighting."

This time I give her a hug before walking back over to Keith.

"Hey baby, you ready?"

"I am." I say taking his hand.

Making it to the car, I lay my head back on the seat.

"Man, I've missed worship."

"Me too." He says. "You want to stop and get something to eat?"

"Maybe later but right now, I am still full from service and all I want is to lay down."

"Are you feeling okay?"

"Just tired."

Twenty minutes later we pull down our street and Dakota's car is parked outside the house.

"Were you expecting her?" I ask Keith.

"No."

He parks in the garage and we both get out.

"Dakota, what are you doing here?" He asks her.

"Why have you blocked my calls like I'm nothing?"

"Are you serious? Look, the moment I found out you were no longer pregnant was the moment we had nothing else to talk about."

"This isn't fair because you didn't let me explain."

"Explain what? You should have told me the truth when you miscarried the baby."

"I COULDN'T!" She yells. "It was the only way to keep you."

2:32AM

"Keep me? I'm not a toy."

"Why am I not good enough for you?"

"Girl, have you lost your last piece of mind? Get the hell off my property." I tell her.

"Oh, Ms. High and Mighty, you think you've won."

"Won what Dakota? This is not a game. Keith is my husband and he has been for the past 19 years. And to think, I was feeling sorry for you. Do you even think you have done anything wrong?"

"Me? I'm wrong?" She yells. "He was mine first and you took him!"

Keith and I look at each other.

"What are you talking about?" Keith asks her.

"I had you first, in college. Tell her!"

Keith

"You are a liar!" I yell.

"Charlotte, you remember the week you left college because your mom was sick?"

"What does that have to do with this?"

"One night I went to a frat party and met Keith. We both got drunk and ended up sleeping together. The next morning, he didn't even remember my name. He threw me out of his bed and the next thing I know, you and he were dating."

"You are a bold face lie!" I scream at her.

"Dakota, why are you doing this?" Charlotte asks.

"Because he is mine, I had him first. Keith, tell her. Tell her the truth so we can be together!" She screams.

He turns to me.

"Babe, the truth is, this chick is crazy and we need to call the police. I swear on my life I never slept with her but the one time."

"I believe you Keith because the week my mom got sick is the same week you spent in Germany. I remember because you wanted to fly home but couldn't so I know she's lying."

"That's not true! He must have come back early." She says.

"Dakota stop! What is wrong with you?"

She starts to cry. "I need him."

"You may need a 'him' but it's not this one." Charlotte says pointing at me. "Now, I've already forgiven you for your disrespect of me and my marriage but I will not stand here and allow you to bring anymore hell on my house. This is the last and final time I'll warn you. Do not come back here again or I will file a restraining order."

We turn to walk in the house with Keith letting the garage down, leaving her standing in the driveway.

"Wow. Do you think we need to go ahead and get a restraining order?" I ask Charlotte.

"We may have too if she comes back."

"Man, I didn't know she was crazy."

"Neither did I," Charlotte says walking to the bedroom. "My mom never liked her but being a fool, I would always stick up for her because she didn't have anybody else. I never thought she'd go to this extreme."

I start undressing but wince in pain.

"You okay?"

"Yea, I just have some pain in my back."

"How long have you had it?"

"I don't know, a few weeks."

"Keith, you know you should have had this checked by now."

"It's probably stress."

"And it's probably not. You need to make an appointment. You haven't had a physical in over a year."

"That's because I'm in great shape." I say flexing my muscles.

"Okay macho man."

"I can show you a macho man."

I grab her and she allows me to kiss her. She pushes me on the bed and straddles me.

After kissing for a minute, I flip her over.

"Are you sure about this?"

"Yes please." She smiles.

I stand up and remove my pants but I have a hard time performing.

"It's okay." She says kissing me.

"No it's not, this has never happened before."

"Do you think something is seriously wrong?"

"I don't know."

"Babe, promise me you'll call the doctor in the morning."

"I will, after your appointment."

"Keith please, this can be serious."

"I will, I promise."

The next morning, I wake up and slip out of bed. Neither of us has to work today because of Charlotte's doctor appointment. Plus she needed to sleep, seeing she was up again at 2:30.

I grab my phone and close our bedroom door. Walking to the living room, I call my doctor's office.

"Yes ma'am, I need to make an appointment. No, I've been there before. 9/11/1980, Keith Hulbert. Yes, that's correct. Um, I'm been having

2:32AM

blood in my urine and some pain in my lower back. Today? What time? Yes, I can make it at 3:30. Thank you."

"You've had blood in your urine?"

I jump at the sound of Charlotte's voice. When I look at her, she has tears in her eyes.

"What aren't you telling me?"

"Babe, it is just stress."

"Keith, it's more than that. Stress will not have you like this."

"I made an appointment for this afternoon. It's not a big deal, stop worrying."

"I, uh--"

"Everything will be okay Charlotte."

Charlotte

"Good afternoon, do you have an appointment."

"I do."

"Your name?"

"Charlotte Hulbert."

"Okay, Mrs. Hulbert, I have you checked in."

Keith and I find a seat and he will not stop fidgeting.

"Babe, stop shaking because you are making me nervous. Here, read a magazine."

I open the kindle app on my phone to start on this new book I downloaded. It's called Her 13th Husband by BM Hardin and this chick is crazy. The character, not the author.

Just when it starts to get really good, the nurse calls my name.

2:32AM

After I am weighed, told to leave a urine specimen and had my vitals taken, we wait for the doctor.

== Knock on the door ==

"Hi, Dr. Meade."

"Hey Charlotte, Keith, how are you both?"

"We're good. How are you?"

"Happy to be on this side of the dirt."

We all laugh.

"Charlotte, has there been any complications since your last appointment?"

"No ma'am, everything has been good."

"Great. You should be around eleven weeks now so I will measure your stomach and listen for the heartbeat. Are you taking your vitamins?"

"Yes ma'am."

"Good. All of your bloodwork came back fine which is great news. Lay back for me."

After she takes measurements of my stomach, she pulls out the Doppler. "Now, we should be able to hear the heartbeat but sometimes, eleven weeks can be too soon so don't worry if we don't,"

She moves the Doppler around until we hear the sound that brings tears to our eyes.

"There it is." Dr. Meade says.

I look over at Keith and his smile is huge.

"Sounds like a pretty healthy heartbeat."

She sits me up.

"Do you have any questions for me?"

"No, none I can think of right now. I don't think the shock of this has worn off yet."

"I understand but enjoy it while you have the chance. Are you experiencing any morning sickness?"

"Not yet, knock on wood."

"Well, you're lucky. Let's pray it stays away. As I told you at your last appointment, your due date is around February 26. On your way out, schedule your next appointment, which will be four weeks. At that time, you will be close to 16 weeks, at which point we will do an ultrasound. However, if you need me in the meantime, do not hesitate to call the office."

"Thank you Dr. Meade."

"You're welcome. See you soon."

Keith kisses the back of my hand before we grab our things and head out, after making my next appointment. When the elevator door opens, Dakota walks out.

"What are you doing here?" She asks looking me up and down.

We try to move around her but she blocks the door.

"Why are you at an OBGYN, you couldn't possibly be pregnant again because we all know how they turn out?"

I close my eyes and count to ten.

"Dakota, you need to move out of the way." Keith says.

"Or what? Are you going to hit me? HUH?" She asks getting loud.

"You seriously need help. Now, move!"

"Oh, face the truth! We all know she can't keep a baby alive." She says laughing.

"You are one sad, pathetic piece of a woman. What did I ever do to you? I was the only friend you had who never judged or hurt you. I took you home with me, when you would have been left at the dorms by yourself. When you didn't have anybody, my family took you in. You spent holidays with us and even went on vacations and this is how you do me. ME! Your best-freaking-friend."

"Yea well, you thought so."

"Babe, let's go. There is no reasoning with someone like her."

"Someone like me! The same somebody you screwed while your wife laid somewhere suicidal." She laughs. "You used to like someone like me boo."

The elevator dings and Keith moves her out the way.

"I pray you find the help you need Dakota."

"SCREW YOU!" She says throwing up the middle finger as the door closes.

"Wow! She is on an entire new level. You don't think she's having some kind of mental break do you?" Keith asks.

"I don't know but if I have too, I will have her arrested."

"We may have too because it's obvious there is something going on but I am not about to worry with her."

"We will figure it out. In the meantime, let's get to your appointment."

"If you're tired, I'll drop you off at home. We have time."

"No sir. I'm going to be there for you just like you're here for me."

2:32AM

Keith

I sign in at the front desk.

"Mr. Hulbert, I need you to update some forms for me." The young lady says, handing me a clip board. I take it right to Charlotte.

"How old are you?" She asks rolling her eyes and snatching the forms from me.

Once she is done with the paperwork, I take it back to the front desk.

"Thank you. Have a seat and the nurse will call you."

We wait about twenty minutes before my name is called.

"Do you want me to wait out here?" Charlotte asks.

"No, I'm okay with you being back there."

"Mr. Hulbert, if you will step on the scale for me?" She writes down my weight. "Okay, follow me."

Once we are in the room, the nurse opens her computer and starts the questioning.

"Mr. Hulbert, what brings you in today?"

"Um, well I've been having some blood in my urine and some pain in my back."

"Okay, how long has it been going on?"

"For a few weeks."

"Is there any history of high blood pressure, heart disease, stroke, diabetes or cancer in your family?"

"My mom has diabetes and my dad had prostate cancer."

"Is your dad still alive?"

"No ma'am, he died three years ago."

"From cancer?"

"Yes."

"Oh, I am sorry." She says typing some additional stuff into the computer. "I'm going to check your vitals."

"Everything looks good. If you can, step out and leave a urine specimen in the bathroom. Put your name on the cup and leave it inside the door. Then you can come back here and the doctor will be in shortly."

By the time I am headed back to the room, the doctor is knocking on the door. I follow him in.

"Hi, I'm Dr. Lawrence."

"Keith and this is my wife Charlotte."

"I know you normally see Dr. Swanson but he's on vacation this week. Now, tell me what brings you in."

I go over the same thing I told the nurse.

"I want to do some tests to see what's going on. What has me concerned is the cancer that runs in your family. Are you up to date on your prostate exams?"

"No, I thought I wouldn't need to start having those until I am 50."

"It is recommend men get tested at 40 and if everything is normal, then again at the age of 50. However, because prostate cancer runs in your family, you are already overdue."

"Do you think I have cancer?"

"I cannot answer, properly, without running the necessary tests. One being a rectal exam to feel for any abnormalities. If there are some, I will have bloodwork done along with an ultrasound and a possible biopsy."

"Wow." I say looking over at Charlotte. Her face is red so I know she's trying to keep from crying.

"Let's not get ahead of ourselves. We will start with the rectal exam and go from there. Would you like your wife to step out?"

2:32AM

"Not unless she wants too." I say looking at Charlotte.

"No, I'm good."

After another thirty minutes, it is decided I need to have an ultrasound and biopsy done immediately. I am scheduled for 8AM, the next morning, at Methodist Hospital in Germantown.

Charlotte and I make it to the car and once inside, we just sit there without saying anything. I start the car and it is quiet the entire ride home.

Pulling into the garage, Charlotte gets out and slams the door.

"Charlotte wait."

She continues to walk, dropping her purse on the island in the kitchen.

"Charlotte, talk to me."

"I begged you to go to the doctor." She says crying. "How many times have I asked you to go and have your physical? How many?"

"I know."

"You know? You know? Look where we are Keith. You can have cancer. I'm pregnant and you can have cancer."

I walk towards her.

"No! Stop. I don't need you to console me. Why is God doing this to us! Haven't we been through enough? Are we just prone to suffer?"

"Baby, calm down."

"It's only been four months, FOUR months, 119 days since we lost Micaela, would He be so cruel to take you too."

I walk closer.

"Baby, don't talk like this."

She begins to hit me in the chest.

2:32AM

"You cannot die on me. You can't! Do you hear me God! I cannot lose my husband. Are you listening?"

When she slides down into the floor, I hold her in my arms.

"I'm scared." She whispers.

"I am too but we will get through this."

"Haven't we suffered enough? Why is God angry at us? What have we done that is bad enough to warrant this? Please tell me and I'll stop. I promise."

I rock her in my arms as she cries.

"Just ask God Keith. Please ask Him and whatever it is, I'll stop."

"God doesn't work that way. We have to trust Him no matter how it turns out."

"I have trusted Him and look where we are. What else am I supposed to do Keith? Just keep praying and hope He shows up in enough time to save you."

"Charlotte, I know you're upset but you have to stop talking like this. Either you trust Him or you don't but as for me, I am placing my life in His hands and whatever He chooses to do, I am okay with it."

"Are you giving up?"

"Heck no but I am giving in. Charlotte, we cannot fight this by ourselves. We tried it before and it did not work. This time, we have to trust God no matter how hard or dark it gets. Promise me, you will not check out on me."

"Kei--"

"Charlotte, promise me."

"I promise."

2:32 AM | August 13, 2017

Blog Title: When Sunday Comes

Its 2:35, I know I am a few minutes late but I almost didn't write tonight because I have so much on my mind.

Then, as I was sitting in the nursery listening to music, a song played. It's an old song by Daryl Coley, titled When Sunday Comes.

It's kind of funny this would be the song to play when I've been sitting here contemplating whether or not I am going to church in a few hours.

I've been having a "Father, can you hear me," moment. Scratch that, month. Child, it feels like every time I am about to make it to the end of trouble, something causes me to stumble again. Then I have to start the process of struggling to pull myself up, all over again.

Anybody else been there?

How many more nights do I have to sit in the floor and call Him and He doesn't answer? How much longer can I survive in the dark, waiting on my morning to show up yet it never comes?

Father, can you hear me?

I want to throw my phone into the wall but I don't. Instead, I allow it to play while I sing along because surely if the singer can believe it, I can too, right?

In the hopes of ministering to someone else this morning, the song says, *"When Sunday comes, my trouble gone. As soon as it gets here, I'll have a new song. When Sunday comes, I won't have to cry no more. Jesus will soothe, my trouble mind and all my heartaches, every burden, all of my misery, all of my crying, every trial, every tribulation will be left behind. When Sunday comes."*

I'm just waiting on Sunday because life is hard, y'all.

So. Very. Hard.

2:32AM

Not only has it been 125 days, 3000 hours, 180,008 minutes since my daughter has been gone but life keeps throwing me daggers and no matter how I try, I cannot seem to dodge them.

But when Sunday comes.

This time, I will not crumble under the pressure. Don't misunderstand me. I want too but I promised my husband I wouldn't lose my faith in God, this time.

Because when Sunday comes.

In the meantime, I am finding my way back to music because if you haven't noticed, music is my release. I lost the feel of it when Micaela died but I realize, it's one of the things which grounds me.

Before I forget, we still haven't unveiled the memorial to our family yet but we will and I promise I'll post pictures for you guys.

For those of you who have left comments this past week, I haven't forgotten about you. I will try to answer as many as I can tomorrow, all I ask is for you to bear with me.

And while you're bearing, please whisper our name in prayer.

Until next time,

Char.

2:32AM

Charlotte

"Hey." I say opening the door to my parents.

"Hey baby, you look tired. Are you okay?"

"Yes mom, I am fine."

"Have you been sleeping?"

"Ruthie, leave the girl alone. Hey Pudding."

"Hey daddy. Y'all come on in. We are waiting on a few of our church members and then we will get started."

"I don't know why you are keeping us in suspense little girl."

"You can wait. Now, go get a drink and calm your nerves lady."

She rolls her eyes. "Where is my son-in-love?"

"He's in the back, he'll be out in a few."

"Is he sick?"

"Ma, please."

"Fine." She says throwing up her hands.

Pastor Donald and Lady Sheree Lawson, along with Angela and her husband Donovan arrives. We were hoping Keith's sister, Karen could make it but she couldn't due to their mom being sick. She has dementia and can't be by herself.

I get everyone settled in the living room as Keith comes in. He grabs my hand and I smile at him before taking our seats.

"Okay everybody, I know you are wondering why we called this impromptu gathering but there are a few things we need to share with you all." Keith says.

"First, before we get into the serious stuff, there is something we want to show you. It's outside in the back."

2:32AM

We all go outside.

"As you all know, it has been a little over four months since Micaela passed away. At first, I didn't think I would survive because the pain of losing a child can sometimes become unbearable but with God's grace, I've made it. We have made it."

I take a breath.

"Since she has been gone, I've started a blog because I am usually up in the early hours of the day but I wanted to do something else to remember her by. So, I had a memorial garden designed in her honor."

Keith pulls the covering from over it.

"Oh Charlotte, it's beautiful." My mom cries as everybody goes over to look at the bench and flowers that have been planted.

"Wow." Angela says wiping tears. "This is amazing."

I wrap my arms around her. We stand out for a minute looking at the garden before heading back inside.

"Can I get anyone something to drink?"

Everyone declines.

"Okay, for the rest of the announcements. I am going to try to get through this without breaking down. All I ask is for you wait until we are done before asking questions. Okay?"

They all nod.

Keith speaks. "I have been diagnosed with advanced Stage 4 prostate cancer. It's advanced because it has spread to my lymph nodes and surrounding tissue. The doctors say it is an aggressive form that has no cure but they have started me on a round of chemotherapy in the hopes of slowing it down. I had my first treatment on Thursday. We don't know if any of this will work but we are trusting God because we--" He stops.

2:32AM

"We know He will get us through this. He has too because we have a baby on the way who has to meet his or her dad."

Everybody's face is a mixture of shock, confusion and happiness.

"We know this is a lot to take in. Trust me, we've been trying to waddle through the heaviness of all this for over a week now. And while I want to break, throw in the towel, give up, cry and yell; it doesn't fix what's broken nor does it stop the storm. So, I am standing because I have to believe God is preparing me, us for something far greater than this. He has to be."

"Charlotte, we can never understand the intimate workings of God. All we can do is trust in the fact, He knows what He is doing." Pastor Lawson says. "I don't know about you all but I believe this is the perfect time to petition God's throne with prayer."

We all stand and grab hands.

"Our Father, holy is your name and may your will be done on earth as it is in heaven. God, we come this afternoon first to tell you thank you. Thank you for the blessings of a new day and thank you for family and friends. Thank you for us being in our right mind and for your many benefits, too numerous to count.

Now, oh master, as we stand around the living room of the Hulbert's, we ask you to come in and sup with us. For we know, when you are in the room, miracles manifest. God, we don't know what your will is but we take you at your word and it says, if we ask it shall be.

So we come now, asking you for the healing of cancer. We know the report of the doctors but we also know your record. We declare total healing and restoration. For you are a God who can calm a raging storm, put a highway through a sea, feed a multitude with two cakes and five sardines, heal the blind, raise the dead and open up closed wombs so surely you can destroy cancer.

2:32AM

Then, don't just stop there because while I got you on the line, I need you to strengthen this mother. God, she's been through enough, count her as favored in your sight. But if she has to suffer like Job, through 41 chapters just to get to the Chapter 42 restoration, then mighty God, give her double the reward. We trust you and shall never take it for granted. By the blood of your son Jesus, we all say together. Amen."

Keith

We spend the next hour with our friends and family, trying to answer the many questions they have. Everybody is, undoubtedly, concerned about us but all we can do is have faith in God.

I walk everybody out before calling out for Charlotte. She doesn't answer.

I walk pass the back door and see her outside, pacing in circles. I open the door but she doesn't hear me, I realize she's praying with tears running down her face.

"God, I know you're listening. I am crying out to you, declaring total healing for my husband. I even declare a healthy life for this baby I am carrying before he or she is birthed into this world. God, your word says you will never leave me nor forsake me, so I am holding you to it for our suffering shall not be in vain. I speak life, not death, healing and not sickness and prosperity not pain. The enemy has no place in our home, our body neither our mind nor soul. I cover every door and window with the blood of Jesus. I speak life!"

When she stops speaking, I walk over to her. She jumps when I touch her arm but immediately begins to speak in tongue while touching every part of my body.

"Life God, not death. Health God, not sickness!" She repeats.

I pull her into me. "Life, not death." She cries out.

I hold her until I feel her body go limp. I pick her up and carry her into the house. Getting her into bed, I go and get a cool towel and place it on her forehead before kneeling next to the bed.

Some hours later, I feel her jump up.

"What time is it?"

"Babe, lay down."

"No Keith, what time is it?"

She reaches toward the nightstand and realize her phone is not there.

"It's 3:45."

"No, I overslept."

"Overslept for what?"

"Micaela."

"Baby, what are you saying?" I ask before realizing she is still asleep but crying.

"Where is she? Keith, where is the baby?"

"Shh, I got you. You're okay."

I pull her to me and she relaxes.

"It hurts, it hurts so much."

I wrap my arms around her and hold her until she falls back to sleep.

The next morning, I open my eyes to see Charlotte is already up. I slowly sit on the side of the bed because it feels like I'm going to be sick. When I stand, the contents of my stomach spill on the floor.

"Babe," Charlotte asks running to me.

"Stay back."

"I will not, let me help you. We knew this could happen."

"I just wasn't expecting it so soon."

She helps me up.

"Go and take a shower while I clean this up."

"You don't have to because I can take care of it once I'm done."

"Boy, go get in the shower. The many times you cleaned up after me when I was pregnant with Micaela. I got this."

Charlotte

I have to hold my breath to keep from throwing up. I didn't want Keith to see me, so I wait until he closes the bathroom door before running to the guest bedroom.

I rinse out my mouth before going to grab a bucket, towels and carpet cleaner from the garage.

By the time I come back, he is coming out of the bathroom.

"Why don't you go and get comfortable on the couch? I'll fix you some toast and ginger tea when I am done."

"You sure you don't want me to help."

"I'm sure."

It takes over 30 minutes to get everything cleaned up. By the time I am done, I have sweated so much that I have to take another shower. When

2:32AM

I come out, Keith is asleep on the couch. I don't wake him, instead I go and fix his toast and tea.

"Babe."

"Hmm." He says without opening his eyes.

"Do you want to try and eat something? I made you some toast."

"Not right now."

I pull the blanket up over him before I grab my computer and head into the nursery. I plug my phone into the speaker and sit in the rocking chair.

The song, Prayer Room by Avery Sunshine begins to play. I close my eyes as the sound of her sultry voice fills the room.

"Somebody called and told me that my friend was in trouble but I was so far away, all I could do was pray. I've been there before, many nights I lay on the floor but I'm singing for you today, only because by the grace. And if they come looking for me, tell them that I'm in my prayer room, praying for you."

I begin to hum with her until she gets to the part which says, "Pray, believe and wait; watch everything get better."

I open up my computer.

2:32 AM | August 22, 2017

Blog Title: Pray, Believe and Wait...

Waiting is the hardest thing anybody has ever had to do, especially when you're waiting on God to move.

Is it hard for anybody else or is it just me?

Yes, I am blogging during the middle of the day. I am surprised at myself. I vaguely remember waking up in the middle of the night but I didn't get up.

My body was tired.

A lot has happened.

I know this is just a blog but I feel close to you all so here goes ... I'm pregnant and my husband has been diagnosed with stage four prostate cancer.

THERE YOU HAVE IT!

How am I doing?

Still surviving breath by breath even though some days it hurts but I promised Keith, I would not turn my back on God again so I am here.

Matter of fact, I am standing, like my grandmother used to say; flat footed and looking the enemy in his funky face because I will not lose my husband.

Not without one hell of a fight.

Anyway, I was listening to the song, Prayer Room, by Avery Sunshine and she says you have to pray, believe, wait and watch everything get better so I'm going to try it.

I am going to pray, believe, wait and watch everything get better for us because the bible says in Isaiah 40:30-31, "Though youths grow weary and tired, And vigorous young men stumble badly, Yet those who wait for the LORD will gain new strength; they will mount up with wings like

2:32AM

eagles, they will run and not get tired, they will walk and not become weary."

So, here's to praying, believing, waiting and watching everything get better.

Will you join with me?

Until next time,

Char.

P.S. I finally unveiled the memorial to my family and they LOVED it. (See pictures below.)

Charlotte

It's been a few weeks since Keith's diagnosis and treatment. Time has been speeding by.

Mom and dad has been a great support as well as our church family. They've been cooking meals and dropping off care packages. Dad has taken over our finances, although we have about six months of savings, he says it is one less thing I have to deal with.

Thank God.

Two weeks ago, I met with Keith's doctors and he said the cancer was not responding to the treatment.

We are not giving up.

His chemotherapy was changed and he has been sicker, which means he has also been meaner.

2:32AM

He was admitted to the hospital on last night because he spiked a fever, which indicates an infection.

The nurse gave him some medication for nausea and pain so he is asleep now. I kiss him on the forehead before I leave for my doctor's appointment.

On the way out of his room, I run into Dr. Mitchell.

"Hey Charlotte, I was starting to worry about you since you've canceled your last few appointments. Is everything okay?"

"I know and I apologize. I should have explained my situation but Keith was diagnosed with cancer and it has been kind of rough."

"Oh Charlotte, I am so sorry. Do you have a few minutes to talk to me now?"

"I have about ten before I have to leave for my doctor's appointment."

"I won't keep you but how have you been coping."

"It has been hard but I'm holding on. I've been journaling and listening to music, which calms me. Oh and I'm pregnant."

"Congratulations. Wow, so many changes can bring an array of emotions. You really should come and see me."

"I will once Keith can get on a regimen that works."

"Is he here in the hospital?"

"Yes. He's in room 582."

"I'll stop by and check on him but come and see me or call and I'll come to you. Being pregnant can cause hormonal changes and added with the stress of a sick spouse--"

"I understand what you're saying and I couldn't agree more. I will call your office on tomorrow to schedule an appointment."

2:32AM

"Great, I'll see you soon. Take care."

"Hey Charlotte, you're by yourself today?"

"Yes, Keith is in the hospital."

"I hope he's okay."

"He has cancer, prostate."

"What grade and stage?"

"Stage four, T4."

"Is he on a hormone therapy?"

"No, they went straight for aggressive chemo."

"What kind?"

"Now he is on Docetaxel, three times a week."

"Is it responding?"

"The first round did not. We were supposed to find out today if this new round is but he got a fever on last night. Dr. Meade, can he survive this?"

She doesn't say anything.

"Please be honest with me. I can take it."

"Charlotte, with his stage and grade, he has a very small chance of survival. The only hope, besides God, is if the cancer responds to the chemo."

"And if it doesn't?"

"Then his chances drastically decrease and the only option is to make him comfortable."

"Oh God."

"I am so sorry Charlotte."

"Thank you for being honest and I am sorry to take up your time with this."

"You don't have to apologize. I am here to help you in any way I can."

She hands me some Kleenex.

2:32AM

"Now, have you had any issues?"

"No, other than a little nausea but it's usually only after Keith gets sick." I laugh.

She laughs too. "What about cramping, spotting or any pain?"

"Nope."

"Great, lay back for me. I'm going to measure the size of your stomach and listen for the heartbeat."

After a few minutes, her face shows concern but she doesn't say anything.

"Is everything okay?"

"You're measuring a little big for sixteen weeks but this isn't abnormal." She reaches in the drawer for the Doppler. "Let's take a listen."

The baby's heartbeat is heard but then she makes a face.

"Dr. Meade, what's wrong?"

"I want to get an ultrasound."

She helps me to sit up on the table.

"Follow me."

She has me wait outside the door while she goes in. After a minute, the door opens.

"Charlotte, you can come in now."

"Hi, my name is Jenna and I'll be performing your ultrasound today. Have you had an ultrasound before?"

"Yes, I've had a few."

"Great then you know what to expect. Lay on the table for me and pull your shirt up. I'll also need you to slide your pants down, just a little. Good."

She lays a towel across the top of my jeans and turns out the light.

"This gel should be warm."

She starts to move the wand around on my stomach. Dr. Meade is looking at the screen and when a smile spreads across her face, I let out the breath I'd been holding.

"Exactly what I thought." She says turning the screen. "You're having twins."

"Twins? Are you sure?" I say beginning to freak out. "Twins? Oh my God, did you say twins?"

"Yep. There's Baby A and here's Baby B."

"Oh my God. Oh my God!"

Jenna and Dr. Meade are laughing.

"Would you like to know the sex?"

"Yes, please."

"Well, this little one is a girl and, oh this one is being stubborn." Jenna says moving my stomach around. "And this one is a boy."

I am crying by now.

"They are identical, which means they share the same amniotic sac."

"Is that a bad thing?"

"No but it means we will need to monitor you a little closer. I will do a few measurements and then I'll print a few pictures for you."

When she is done, she wipes the jelly from my stomach before helping me off the table to fix my jeans.

"Here are your pictures. Congratulations mommy." Jenna says.

"Your due date is February 26 but with multiples, you may not carry to full term. I want to see you back in two weeks instead of four. Make sure you stay hydrated and nourished. You're eating for three now. As always, if you need me outside of business hours, don't hesitate to call."

2:32AM

Keith

"I open my eyes but Charlotte isn't there. I get ready to push the button for the nurse, when she walks through the door.

"Hey you. You okay?"

"Yea, I had a doctor's appointment. Are you okay?"

"Just a little thirsty."

She grabs me some water and holds the straw to my lips.

"Is the baby okay?" I ask when she is done wiping my mouth.

"Um, there isn't a baby."

"What do you mean?"

"There are two."

My eyes widen as she pulls out the ultrasound pictures.

"Are you kidding?"

"Um, no boo; you impregnated me with two this time."

"Double the reward." I say.

"Huh?"

"You remember when Pastor Lawson prayed, at the house? He said if you had to suffer through 41 chapters like Job to get to his Chapter 42 blessing, to give you…"

"Double the reward." We both say together.

"What does this mean?" She asks

"It means our suffering isn't over."

She turns away from me and walks over to the window.

"Charlotte, don't shut me out. What are you thinking?"

"I don't know what I'll do if I were to lose you."

"You will live."

"Keith, this isn't fair."

"Babe, whoever told you life was fair? Even as good as we desire it to be, life can sometimes deal us a bad hand. It doesn't mean we forfeit the game but we may have to throw it in, start over and keep playing until we win. And sometimes, winning doesn't happen on earth but it does in eternity."

When I see the tears falling from her eyes, I reach out my hand to her. She slides in the bed with me.

"Charlotte, I'd never leave you if I had a choice but this, it's out of my hands. But if me dying, in this body, gives you double reward; I'll gladly lay my life down."

I feel her body shaking from crying.

"We just have to trust that God knows what He's doing. Will you do that, for me?"

"I'm trying." She whispers.

"Sing for me."

"I can't."

"Please."

She sits up.

"Sing the song you were playing last night."

She stands back up and as the tears continue, she opens her mouth ...

"Sometimes it feels cold and you feel all alone but hold on, better days are coming. It can be rough in this world, I know it ain't easy but hang on in there; I know better days are coming."

I was so caught up in Charlotte that neither of us heard the door open. When I hear someone sniff, I turn to see a couple of nurses and Dr. Mitchell.

2:32AM

Charlotte is repeating, better days are coming and when she breaks, Dr. Mitchell grabs her.

When they slide down onto the floor, Dr. Mitchell rocks her and then she begins to pray.

"God, our Father, we stand in need of your touch for we know your touch can make everything alright. God, I am not asking you to remove the pain but give power to press until you say it's done. I'm not asking you to stop the suffering but give strength until their sorrow is satisfied. I'm not asking you to stop their tears but comfort until you wipe them away. God, I'm not even asking you to remove the darkness but will you give them night time vision until morning shows up. Please oh God, not just by my faith but connected with the faith of all those who stand in agreement. Amen."

I spend the next four days in the hospital. Due to the aggressiveness of the chemotherapy, the side effects have been harsh. It has caused some wild mood swings, depression, crying and a whole lot of pain.

Yet Charlotte has been right by my side. Even when I lash out, all she does is hold me or she sings. I know it is nothing and nobody but God sustaining us.

"Hey babe, you okay?"

"Yeah." I say wiping my face.

"Why are you crying, are you in pain?"

"A little but come and sit for a second because I need to talk to you."

"Okay, let me grab your tea."

"No, it can wait."

"What's wrong?" She asks, looking worried, while sitting on the ottoman in front of me.

2:32AM

"I want to apologize to you."

"What have I told you about apologizing for doing what I am supposed to do?"

"I know but I've taken my frustration out on you and you don't deserve it."

"Babe, you're sick and in pain. A pain I couldn't begin to imagine so if I have to deal with your mood swings, I will. God knows you've had to put up with mine."

"And look how that turned out, I cheated. Are you going to cheat to?"

"Now, you're talking silly. You know I will never do that. Keith, with everything we've had to deal with since the beginning of the year, my skin has gain some toughness. So if you can handle the side effects of chemo, surely I can handle the side effects of you."

"I'm tired." I tell her.

"Then lay down and rest. We can talk later."

"No Charlotte, I am tired of the doctors, the chemo, not being able to eat because the food taste funny and not having the ability to keep down what I do eat. I can't even make love to you anymore."

"You will again."

"We don't know that and we have to be realistic."

"Keith, I am not about to sit here and listen to you talk like this. You promised you would fight."

"And I have."

"But it's only been a couple of months."

"You don't think I know that?" I say louder than I expected. "I'm sorry, I didn't mean to yell. Look, I am not talking about giving up today. If it is God's will, I pray He allows me to at least see our babies be born."

2:32AM

"And then what? You get to kiss all of us goodbye?"

"Not goodbye but goodnight."

Charlotte

I can't say anything.

"Tell me what you're thinking."

My leg begins to shake.

"Baby, don't shut me out."

"Keith, I want to be selfish and ask you to fight more but how can I? I know the amount of pain you're in. Yes, I want to watch you with our children but what quality of life will that be if all you have to look forward to is treatment and side effects. I don't want to lose you but I will not ask you to unnecessarily suffer."

He grabs my hand.

"If the cancer isn't responding, we will talk to the doctor and figure out a plan, okay?"

I nod and force a smile.

"Do you want your tea now?" I ask him.

2:32AM

"No, I'm going to lay down for a minute."

I wait until he is settled on the couch before I walk out in the back yard. I need to scream and I didn't want him to worry.

I go into his shed and begin to pace. When I notice a box of tiles, from the bathroom floor he'd remodeled; I begin to throw them against the wall.

"WHY ME?" I scream.

Glass shattering.

"WHY DO I HAVE TO SUFFER THIS BAD?"

More glass breaking.

"HAVE I NOT DONE ENOUGH?"

When I am out of breath and tiles to break, I begin to speak in tongue to the Lord.

Then I hear a voice saying, Job 38.

At first, I want to be stubborn but when I hear the voice again, I leave out of the shed and head back to the house.

I walk into the bedroom and grab Keith's bible from his nightstand. Flipping it to Job 38, I begin to read out loud.

"Then the Lord answered Job from the whirlwind: "Who is this that questions my wisdom with such ignorant words? Brace yourself like a man, because I have some questions for you and you must answer them."

I continue to read and the more I do, the more convicted I begin to feel.

And when I get to Job 42, I begin to read out loud again but this time, Job's words became my prayer from a repentant heart.

"I know you can do anything, and no one can stop you. You asked, 'who is this questioning my wisdom with such ignorance?' It is I—and I was talking about things I knew nothing about, things far too wonderful for me. You said, 'Listen and I will speak! I have some questions for you, and you must answer them.' I had only heard about you

2:32AM

before, but now I have seen you with my own eyes. I take back everything I said, and I sit in dust and ashes to show my repentance."

"Forgive me oh God."

2:32 AM | October 6, 2017

Blog Title: Dear Micaela

It has been 149 days since I've held you, rocked you or kissed your sweet face. 149 days of restless nights and questions of why. 149 days, most of which have consisted of tears.

My dearest Micaela, mommy misses you with every beat of my heart. You'd be nine months now; sitting up, rolling over, making noises and probably even crawling. You'd have daddy wrapped around your little finger and me too.

We miss you.

But guess what, you're going to be a big sister to a baby brother AND a baby sister. I know, right. I still haven't fully grasped the news.

Anyway, Daddy is sick and the doctors say his body isn't responding to any of the therapies

2:32AM

they've tried. They want to try an experimental trial but I don't know if he even has the strength.

He is trying to be strong for me but I know his body is tired and he doesn't want to spend the last of his days being sick.

Ugh, everything is so hard lately but we're going to make the best of the time we have left.

Rest on my sweet girl until I see you in Heaven.

Until next time,

Mommy.

Keith

"Babe, are you ready?"

"I'm coming." I say dragging my suitcase from the bedroom. "Do you have everything you need?"

"Yes, I am all packed just waiting on you."

"Then let's go."

Charlotte and I are flying to see my mom and sister in Cincinnati. I wanted to tell her face to face about my decision to stop treatment.

Karen, my sister, is the caretaker for my mom and she doesn't like leaving her with anybody else. Mom suffers from dementia and although she has days where she's lucid, over this past year she has more days when she is not which means she has to be watched carefully.

2:32AM

"You okay?" Charlotte ask covering my hand. "The plane ride isn't making you sick is it?"

"No, nothing like that."

"Then what has you worried? I can see it all over your face."

"I haven't seen mom since her dementia got worst and now she may not recognize me. I should have come when Karen called."

"Babe, stop beating yourself up. You had no way of knowing your mom's sickness would progress this fast."

"Like mine?"

"Keith--"

"It's okay, I take the blame for what my stubbornness caused."

She smiles at me.

I put my headphones in and lay my head back.

"Keith?"

"Hmm."

"Come on babe, we're landing."

I open my eyes and realize I've slept the entire flight.

"You feel okay?"

"Yes. What about you?" I ask rubbing her stomach.

"We're fine. I'm just worried about you."

"Stop worrying babe, I am good. I promise."

Once we get our bags and rental car, we make the thirty minute drive to my sister's house. I sent her a text before we left the airport, so she had the door open for us.

"Karen?" I call out, stepping through the front door.

"In the kitchen."

2:32AM

Charlotte and I round the corner and there are cousins, aunts and uncles.

"Big brother!" Karen yells running to me. "I am so happy you're here."

"Me too." I say squeezing her a little longer.

"Charlotte, wow, look at this belly."

I watch the joy in my sister's face at seeing us, knowing I have to break the news of me dying, sooner.

"Come on in because everybody is here for you."

"Where's mom?"

"Over there with Aunt Leslie."

I walk over to her and she's looking out the window. I kneel down and touch her leg. When she turns, her face lights up.

"Oh Keith! God told me you were coming."

I hug her.

"Yes mom, it's me."

"You've come to say goodbye, haven't you?"

I lower my head.

"It is okay, God told me you're sick and He also told me your healing won't come on this side but you know that already, don't you?"

"Yes ma'am," I say with tears in my eyes.

The room has gotten so quiet, I can hear my heart beating.

"That's alright, you know. When we leave this world, we sleep in God's perfect peace until the time He comes back for us. So don't you be afraid of dying. There ain't nothing wrong with dying when you know where you're going. Now, you got a problem if you don't. I know where I'm going when these old eyes close and that's why I told God, whenever He's ready for me, I'm ready for Him."

I wipe the falling tears. "Yes ma'am."

2:32AM

"And stop worrying about that girl and those babies because they will be alright. You hear me?" She says lifting my head. "She's made it right with God and He's covering her. She has to suffer because nobody is exempt but she's strong and she will survive. Your son and daughter will make you proud, too. So, stop blaming yourself. You're stubborn just like your daddy was, God rest his soul. "

I look back at Charlotte who is standing arm in arm with Karen and they are both crying.

I lay my head on her leg and cry.

"Everything is going to be just fine." She says turning to look back at the window. "God said so."

When I raise my head, I call her name.

"Mom?"

"I'm ready for a nap. Are you my new nurse? What's your name?" She asks looking at me as though it's our first time meeting.

"I got her." Aunt Leslie says.

When she's gone, Karen comes over followed by my cousins and uncle.

"Is it true? You're dying?"

"Yes."

"You told me you were sick, not dying."

"I know and I'm sorry. I couldn't tell you over the phone."

"No Keith!" She says hitting me. "No, you cannot die on me."

I grab her arms and pull her into me.

"You can't die, you just can't."

"I am so sorry."

2:32AM

Charlotte

I slide out of bed, quietly as to not wake Keith. I take my phone and slip out of the bedroom, headed down to the kitchen.

I jump when I see Karen at the refrigerator.

"Oh God, you scared me." She says. "You couldn't sleep either?"

"No, my sleep hasn't been right since Micaela died."

"I'm sorry I haven't been there for you guys."

"Karen, with everything you have going on here, don't you dare apologize. Being a caretaker is a hard job."

She sighs. "It is and you know, firsthand, because you've become one for my brother."

"Yeah and we both know how men can be when they are sick."

"Whiny babies."

We both laugh.

"Seriously Charlotte, how are you?"

"I'm surviving one breath at a time."

"I've never heard that before."

"Well, it hurts too much to deal with the pain in hours, days and weeks, so I settle for breaths."

"I hear that. You want some warm milk?"

"Sure."

She goes over to get a pot out of the cabinet just as my phone dings.

"Everything okay?"

"Yea, it's a message from my blog."

"You blog now?"

"Yea, I started it when I would be up in the mornings."

"What is it about?"

"Mostly the pain of losing Micaela."

"Cool. What's the name of it?"

"2:32AM."

"That's an odd name."

"It's the time I found Micaela in her crib."

"Oh Charlotte, I am so sorry."

"Don't be, I've gotten better at dealing with it."

"But isn't it hard to think about?"

"Everything is but I've found blogging and journaling to be a release for me although I haven't been able to do a lot of it lately."

She gets some cups from the cabinet and pours the milk in them. Handing me one, she looks like she wants to say something.

"What is it?"

"You don't have to answer if you don't want but how were you able to take my brother back after he cheated on you?"

"It wasn't easy, trust me but Keith and I have been together over 19 years. He's all I've ever known when it comes to a man. We've, essentially, grown up together and although I could have; I didn't want to start over without him."

"Sister, here's to you," she says clinking our glasses together. "Couldn't have been me. I would have beaten his black ass."

"Oh, I wanted too." I chuckle.

"Do you think Keith getting sick is God's way of punishing him for cheating on you?"

I shake my head while taking a sip of the milk. "God doesn't work that way. If He did, there would be a lot more people sick and/or dead. Keith's sickness is just that, a sickness and there is no way we could have predicted it happening."

"But everything is happening so quickly."

2:32AM

"I know but we have to trust it is all God's plan."

"What are you two talking about?" Keith asks.

"Hey babe, you okay?"

"Yea, I was coming to get some water but since my sister is up, I want to talk to her."

"Okay. I'll be in the bedroom."

Keith

"You want some warm milk?"

"You still drink that? Momma used to make it for us when we were small."

"I know but it helps me to sleep."

"Well, come and talk with me for a minute."

She comes over and sits across from me.

"Karen, I know you're upset with me but I didn't want to tell you about my decision to stop treatment, over the phone."

"But why would you stop when it could prolong your life?"

"It is not a guarantee besides what kind of life could I have tied to a bed all day or gripping a toilet from throwing up even when there is nothing in my stomach?"

2:32AM

"We could have gotten you some marijuana or something."

"Marijuana?"

"I read it can help cancer patients."

I laugh and she starts to cry.

"Don't cry."

"What am I going to do without you? Mom is sick and we don't know how much longer she has then it'll just be me."

"You have Aunt Leslie, Uncle Washington and all your cousins. Plus Charlotte and the babies."

"It's not the same."

"I know but you have to know I would fight if there was a chance it would help."

"You don't know because you didn't try."

"I did, you have to believe I would never give up without a fight. Now, stop crying because I need you to do something for me."

"What?" She ask wiping her face with the end of her shirt.

"I left something for Charlotte in your room. Everything you'll need is in the box. Make sure she gets it but only after I'm gone."

"Why didn't you just give it to her?"

"You'll understand when you see it. Just promise me you will take care of it."

"Of course I will."

"Thanks. Now give me a hug."

"I'm still mad at you."

"You can be mad all you want until we get ready to leave."

"I can't say goodbye."

"Then don't, say goodnight because I'll see you again."

2:32AM

Karen and I stay up watching movies, laughing and talking until the sun comes up. Something we haven't done since we were teenagers.

A few days later, Charlotte and I prepare to leave. I give Karen a hug, holding her a little longer and tighter. Mom didn't recognize me but it didn't stop me from giving her one last kiss.

TWO DAYS LATER

"Hey Keith, how are you feeling today?"

"I'm okay Dr. Baker, just a little tired."

"How about your pain, on a scale from one to ten?"

"Maybe a five right now."

"Are you sleeping?"

"When I can."

"When I asked you before, you said no to a clinical trial but have you changed your mind? There's one starting in Baltimore on November 13th. It's a three to six month trial and although it will not cure you, it can possibly add six more months to your life."

"That's next week."

2:32AM

"I know but I just got word of them having a space for you."

"What will I have to do?"

"You'll have to move there until the trial is over so they can manage how your body reacts. You'll spend most of the day being tested--"

I stop him. "Dr. Baker, I don't mean to cut you off but what if I don't do the trial, how much longer do you believe I will live?"

"With the cancer being in your bones and lymph nodes, three to six months max, give or take a week."

I look over at Charlotte who is very quiet.

"Baby, what do you think?"

"Keith, I support whatever you want. You are the one who has to deal with the tests, medications and side effects; not me. Whatever you decide, I'm with you. If you want to move to Boston, we will be on the next plane. If it isn't, we will continue making memories."

I look back at Dr. Baker.

"Doc, I appreciate you thinking about me, in regards to the trial and while it may give me six more months, all I need is three to see my wife give birth to my son and daughter."

"Are you sure? It's worth a try."

"Maybe for somebody else but not me. I don't want to take the chance of going to Baltimore and the medicine confining me to a hospital bed during Thanksgiving. No thanks, I have had enough."

"I already knew what you'd say but I had to offer. As you know, I will turn your care over to our hospice team. Once you're under hospice, you will no longer need to come back and forth to this office. Whatever you need, they will take care of."

"Thank you Dr. Baker for all of your help. You have been a true blessing to me and my wife."

2:32AM

"You're welcome. I'm just sorry I wasn't able to cure you."

"You didn't have the authority because my cure was already set before any of this even began. My healing will come, on God's time."

Charlotte

I get Keith in the car and before I can get my seatbelt on, my phone rings with a call from my dad.

I press the answer button on the steering wheel.

"Hey daddy."

"Hey Pudding, how are you?"

"I'm good, just leaving the doctor with Keith."

"Oh okay, I will not hold you long but you remember the clients from Happy Baby?"

"Yea."

"They are still interested in interviewing you."

"I don't know Dad, there is so much going on."

2:32AM

"Do it." Keith says.

I don't say anything.

"Dad, she'll do it."

I look at Keith.

"You have too."

"Fine, I'll do it."

"Great. Let me know a good time you can come and meet them."

"Wait, can they not come to the house?"

"Are you comfortable with that?"

"Yeah. How soon can it be done?"

"One second and I'll find out."

He puts me on hold. "What about Wednesday afternoon, about three."

"That works."

"Great. Nadia, from Happy Baby will call you with the information."

I release the call and look at Keith.

"What?"

"Do you really think I'll be able to do this?"

"Charlotte, you are one of the strongest women I know so I have no doubt you'll be able to do it. Besides, there are other women depending on you and you've never even met them."

I give him one last look before fastening my seatbelt and pulling off.

The next day I go for my prenatal checkup.

"Hey Charlotte. How are you feeling?" Dr. Meade inquires.

"I am doing well. Just tired."

"That's to be expected. You're 25 weeks now with twins but I will have some blood drawn, before you leave, to check your A1C and iron levels."

"Okay."

"Do you have any questions or concerns?"

"Just one."

"Lay back and let me take some measurements while you ask."

"Do you think I will carry the babies' full term?"

"We can never be too sure with twins. Why do you ask?"

"Keith has decided to stop his cancer treatment."

"Oh Charlotte." She states, sympathetically.

"The doctor said, on yesterday, he may have three to six months left and I want to make sure he is here to see the babies take their first breath."

She sits me up.

"Charlotte, I wish I could tell you the easy answer but I can't. Your body will tell you when it's ready to deliver these two however, it is my hope they stay put until at least 36 weeks. I will also pray

Keith is here to see it but we know it is not a guarantee."

"I know."

"Any more questions?"

"No."

"Then I will let you go and sign in at the lab to have some blood drawn. I will see you in two weeks. Have a Happy Thanksgiving."

"You too Dr. Meade."

2:32 AM | November 15, 2017

Blog Title: Happy Baby

Its 2:32am. I know, I know. It's been a while since I've blogged at this hour but I'm up. Mostly because I am nervous about an interview I have to do tomorrow with a company called Happy Baby.

They are raising awareness about SIDS and they've asked to interview me. With everything going on, I wanted to decline but my husband says I need to do it, for all the mothers who have experienced the pain of losing a precious son or daughter but more so for those who haven't.

God knows, this is a pain I wouldn't wish on anybody and if my babbling for twenty minutes helps to prevent someone else from feeling this, I'll do it.

I'm still nervous though.

Man, if only I could have a glass of wine.

Oh, just to give you a little update. The babies are growing and healthy. They are due February 26 but with multiples, it could be early.

My husband, Keith, is still very sick. I will not go into much detail only to ask for your continued prayers.

We know God has the final say and we are standing on that. Even when I want to scream and be mad, I am learning to trust God. I lost my faith once, I am not willing to lose it again.

Has it been hard? Of course. If you saw my husband's shed, you'd know exactly how hard. (Don't ask.)

Anyway, wish me luck and whisper our names in prayer.

Until next time,

Char.

2:32AM

Charlotte

Wow! I didn't know it took so much to get a twenty minute interview. The crew has been here since 6AM, transforming my living room into a studio, of sorts.

They have to make sure the light is right and with good sound. I gave them a tour of the house and also allowed them to take pictures of Micaela's memorial garden and nursery.

Now, as I sit in hair and makeup, I am beginning to feel the heaviness of this assignment.

"Can you all give me a minute?"

"Yes ma'am."

I get up and walk into the guest room where Keith is.

His eyes are closed so I turn to leave when he calls out.

"Hey you."

"Hey, I didn't mean to wake you."

"What's wrong?"

"I don't know if I can do this." I say with tears filling my eyes.

He slides over a little and pats the bed.

I grab a towel from the nightstand and lay it over him to keep from getting makeup on his shirt.

"Maybe I am not the right person for this."

"Who is?" He asks.

"Somebody whose pain isn't so fresh."

"Does the pain ever stop being fresh, though?"

I sigh.

"But what do I say?"

"You say whatever God puts on your heart. If you do, then it has no choice but to reach the hearts of those who need to hear it. Babe, everything we've gone through has been for a purpose and maybe this is it."

"I wish He would have picked a better way to tell me."

"Then you may have missed it."

"When did you get so wise?"

"Pain has a way of doing that. Now, go out there and make me proud."

I smile at him before giving him a kiss. "I'll let you rest because I know all of the noise hasn't allowed you too."

"Girl, with this medicine, I could sleep through a tornado."

"I'll be back." I reply laughing.

"And I'll be waiting."

Before I have my makeup finished, I go into our bedroom and close the door.

"Okay God. You have me here for a reason so I need you to show up because I cannot do this without you. Increase in me so when I speak, it is from you. Strengthen me so I don't stutter in my words or lose my train of thought but use me to encourage others while edifying you. There are too many grieving and in a dark place. There are too many who feel suicidal because death has shown up. Use my voice to let them know, there is joy after this. Even while I'm still in my storm, use me to help somebody else. In your name I pray. Amen."

Interview

"Good evening and welcome to the Happy Baby Channel. I am your host Nadia Grant and my guest today is Mrs. Charlotte Hulbert. Mrs. Hulbert, thank you so much for agreeing to sit down with us."

"Thank you for having me."

"As you know, here at Healthy Baby, our goal is to help moms and dads, across the world, raise healthy and happy babies. This is why today's interview on SIDS is so crucial. I know you recently lost your daughter to SIDS and with it being only a few months, tell me why you agreed to speak to us today."

"To be honest Nadia, I don't know why I agreed but I do know SIDS is an important topic. Yes, my daughter passed away 189 days ago, on April 10 at 2:32am and it's a morning I'll never forget. My speaking cannot prevent SIDS but if my story can help another mother and father get through this difficult time, who am I to remain quiet."

"Did you know about SIDS before it happened to your daughter?"

"Yes, I knew a little about it. I mean, I read about it in books and I thought we were taking all of the necessary precautions, putting her to sleep on her back, not having items around her and such but it still took her."

"How are you so strong right now?"

"This isn't strong, this is me surviving one inhale and exhale at a time."

"I've never heard it said like this before."

"I have realized, at any moment, life can change leaving the following minutes, hours and days hard to bear so I stopped counting the minutes and started appreciating the breaths."

2:32AM

"What do you say to others who are dealing with this?"

"Three things. Don't give up, don't allow someone to tell you how long to grieve and seek help if you need it."

"Did you seek help? If it is too personal, you do not have to answer."

"I don't mind but yes. I started to see a therapist because I knew there was no way I could make it through on my own. I was so angry with God that I began losing faith in Him and had it not been for therapy, I probably wouldn't be in the right frame of mind to sit here, now."

"What are some of the other things you have used or done to help yourself to cope?"

"You mean besides anger?" I laugh. "Therapy has been one of the biggest help. I started a blog and it helps. I sing because music has always been my safe place and I journal. My therapist, Dr. Mitchell, gave me a journal titled Heroine Addict.

It talks about helping you become addicted to the strong and courageous woman you are. I'm sorry, am I taking too much time."

"Oh no, please continue."

"In this journal, the author breaks down the letters of heroine. H-E-R-O-I-N-E. The h stands for habitable and she says our bodies have to be a place the Holy Spirit can inhabit. Mine used to be but then death happened and it made me angry. I found myself up, most mornings, at 2:32am, hence the blog and it made me realize just how much my anger was keeping me from God."

"Wow." Nadia says.

"Nadia, I don't have all the answers when it comes to how to cope with losing a child but I'm trying. Yes, there are days I still scream out to God, days I break things and shut people out and cry but those are my ways of dealing along with everything else. They may not work for anybody else but they work for me."

2:32AM

"Charlotte, we thank you for taking the time to speak with us. Here at Happy Baby, we want to equip you with the information and tools to raise happy and healthy babies. To read more about Micaela's story, log on to our website where you will find the link to Charlotte's blog and more information on this journal. Until next time."

"And cut!" The producer says.

"Was this okay?"

"It was great. We will use some of the pictures your father gave us as well as those we took today. Once we edit the video, you will get a copy to proof before it goes live."

"Thank you."

"No, thank you. Can I give you a hug?"

"Of course."

2:32 AM | November 24, 2017

Blog Title: Thankfulness

It's 2:32am and I am up. I thought I was getting over this part of grief. You know the kind that keeps snatching you out of your sleep. Nonetheless, here I am.

This morning though, I am sitting next to Keith's bed. His pain has gotten worse over the past two weeks so his hospice doctor has increased his dosage which makes him sleep a lot more. He has some good days but reality is starting to sink in he may not make it to see the New Year.

God knows I am grateful for the time I've gotten to spend with Keith but watching him die is harder than losing Micaela. Each time I walk through the door, I am fearful of finding him gone.

Thankfulness.

2:32AM

This is the word that keeps popping in my head and as much as I want to ask, "What do I have to be thankful for," I cannot. Even in the midst of this sorrow, I still have a lot to be thankful for.

I am thankful for my parents who relocated their Annual Thanksgiving dinner here so we could all be together.

I am thankful for Keith's family, especially his sister, who tried to get his mom here but couldn't because she freaked out on the plane.

I am thankful for our church family, who began to stream worship service live, just so we can watch it from the house.

I am thankful y'all. Even though every part of me hurts, I am thankful. Even though the darkness has lingered longer than I want, I am thankful. And even though the enemy has overstayed his welcome, I am still thankful.

What about you? On this early black Friday morning, what are you thankful for?

Before I leave you, let me share with you what Keith said he was thankful for. I wrote it in my journal after dinner and now I am sharing it with you because putting it in writing, will keep me from forgetting.

"I am thankful for everything, the good and the bad. The bad because it makes me appreciate the good. Charlotte, I am thankful for your forgiveness. Without you, I don't know how I would have made it. To mom and dad, thank you for loving me like a son. Although I have made some mistakes, you didn't judge me. And I am thankful for God's promise and if I don't live to see another thanksgiving, I am grateful for the many we've had the chance to share."

Thankfulness.

Until next time,

Char.

2:32AM

Charlotte

We are nine weeks away from delivering the babies and our prayer is for Keith to hold on long enough to see them. We had another ultrasound on yesterday and they are both doing great, plus we were able to see the babies in 3D.

I don't know who was crying the most, me or Keith but seeing them made me finally take down Micaela's crib. I couldn't bear to throw it out so it's in the attic.

The two new cribs, I ordered, for the twins were delivered last week. Keith wanted to be the one to put them together but his energy level wouldn't allow it. Instead, I asked Connor, the one who built the memorial in the back yard, if he could.

He said yes. He even used Keith's help, when he was able.

"Hey you."

"Hey, how do you feel? Are you in pain?" I ask him closing my journal.

"A little."

"You want to take something?"

"No, I am too tired to sleep. It sounds crazy but it's true. Anyway, what are you writing?"

"Just stuff." I smile.

He holds out his hand. "Come lay with me."

"With all this?" I ask rubbing my growing belly.

"Yes, all this."

"Okay, don't say anything when I take up all your space."

"I won't."

It takes a minute but I finally get comfortable next to him.

2:32AM

"Babe, isn't it crazy Christmas will be here in less than two weeks?"

"It's December, already?" He asks.

"December fourteenth, to be exact."

He sighs. "The saying is true, time waits for no man."

"It certainly does not." I tell him.

"Speaking of time, we need to choose names for the babies?"

"Oh no, I did my part and named the boy, you have to pick hers."

"That's not fair because his was easy."

"I know." I laugh. "Keith Oliver Hulbert, Jr."

"Well Ms. Smarty, I've already picked her name too."

"Oh, you have? Then let's hear it."

"Kia Grace Hulbert."

"Kia Grace?"

"Yeah, Virginia helped me pick it out the other night. Kia means new beginnings and Grace comes from the Latin word meaning God's favor."

"Wow babe," I say trying not to cry. "It is both perfect and sad all at the same time."

I groan in pain.

"I guess they like it too." I say rubbing my stomach.

"You okay?"

"Yea, it's just Braxton Hicks."

"You sure?" He asks.

"Oh!"

"Babe, we need to get you to the hospital."

"I'm good. I've been having them off and on for about a week now. Dr. Meade said it's normal. I'm going to walk around to see if they stop."

As soon as I stand up, another pain hits me. I cry out just as Virginia, Keith's nurse comes in.

2:32AM

"Mrs. Charlotte, are you in labor?"

"No, it's too early. I am only 31 weeks."

I cry out again.

"Come, let's get you to the hospital. Is your bag packed?"

"Yes, it's in the hall closet."

"Okay, I'll grab it while you get your shoes. Mr. Keith, you wait here and I will get your wheelchair."

Two hours later, I am hooked up to a fetal monitor and IV. Dr. Meade ordered some medication to stop the contractions and so far, it seems to be working.

"Babe, let Virginia take you home."

"I don't want to leave you."

"I'll be okay. Mom and Dad are on the way and I know you're hurting because I can see it on your face."

"Let me take you home, Mr. Keith. We can FaceTime Mrs. Charlotte before you go to sleep." Virginia says.

"You'll call me if there is any change?"

"Of course, I will."

Virginia helps him to stand so he can give me a kiss.

"I'll see you soon."

Keith

"Are you comfortable?" Virginia asks when she gets me settled in the bed.

"I am."

"Are you ready for your pain medicine?"

"Not yet, I want to talk to Charlotte first."

"Okay, here is your phone. I'll be back in about ten minutes."

When she leaves, I call Charlotte.

"Hi babe, how are you feeling?" She asks when the video connects.

I make a face that causes her to laugh.

"Okay, Mr. Comedian, have you had your pain medicine for the night?"

"Not yet, I wanted to talk to you first."

"Well, Dr. Meade just left and she gave me a steroid shot, to help with their lungs, just in case the labor progresses. But as long as the contractions do not start back, I'll be able to come home in the morning." She says yawning. "She knows I need to be there with you."

"Babe."

She gets quiet.

"Charlotte, I know you're worried about me but don't be. I need you to be strong for the babies."

"I will, if you promise to give me a little more time with you."

This time I get quiet trying not to cry.

"I wish I could make you that promise." I reply.

"I know and I am sorry for even asking it. We will take whatever time God gives us. Besides, for all we know, God can give you a life sentence when man has declared death. That's faith right?"

"Faith is the substance of things hoped for, evidence of things not seen but we also have to be realistic. If God doesn't heal me on this side, faith in Him still has power. You know this right?"

"I do."

"Good." I say when Virginia walks in.

"Are you ready for your medicine Mr. Keith?"

"I am, hold on babe."

When Virginia is done, I pick the phone up.

"I'll be right outside if you need anything." She says turning out the light.

"I hope you didn't fall asleep." I say to Charlotte.

"No, I'm here."

"Do you remember the nights, in college, we'd stay up talking on the phone until we fell asleep?"

"Yea, you would always be the first one to go."

"Because you would be singing. I couldn't help but fall asleep."

"Are you saying my singing sucked?"

I laugh.

"What was the name of the song you used to have me sing all the time?" She asks me.

"Ribbon in the sky?" I say, remembering like it was yesterday. "It was the first dance at our wedding. I can't believe you didn't remember it."

"Boy that was almost 20 years ago."

"I always thought we'd get to renew our vows for our 20th anniversary so we could dance to the song again."

"Me too."

"You know what that means, don't you?"

"What?"

2:32AM

"You have to sing it for me."

"Now? No babe, I can't."

"Sing it now or at my funeral."

She rolls her eyes. "That's not fair, with your ugly self because you know I'll never be able to do it."

"Then you better start Mrs. Hulbert."

"You're so wrong."

"Sing woman!"

She clears her throat.

"Oh so long, for this night I prayed that a star would guide you my way. To share with me this special day, well a ribbon's in the sky for our love. If allowed may I touch your hand and if pleased may I once again, so that you too will understand--"

Charlotte

I continue to sing until I hear Keith snoring. I lay the phone on my chest and cry. I don't release it because I want to listen to him breathe, for as long as I can.

The next morning Dr. Meade stopped by to say she wanted to keep me here because my amniotic sack was leaking. It hasn't completely broken yet but just to be on the safe side.

She gave me another dose of steroids and medication for infection.

I call Keith but Virginia answers.

"Hey Mrs. Charlotte."

"Hey Virginia, is he still asleep?"

"Yes ma'am, this morning has been kind of rough in the pain department. How are you?"

2:32AM

"I'm okay." I tell her before giving her an update on what Dr. Meade said.

"I will let him know as soon as he wakes up. I'm sure, if he's able, we will be there to see you."

"I am sure. Thank you Virginia. You have been a God send."

"You are welcome. Now, get some rest."

The rest of the afternoon crawled by. Mom and Dad stopped by with some food because this bland hospital food was not cutting it. They stayed and kept me company for a little while but now, I am here alone.

With my thoughts.

Virginia text to say Keith was in too much pain to travel today although I did get a chance to see him open his eyes and he blew me a kiss.

Mane, cancer sucks!

I pull out my journal and stop on the page that has a verse. I didn't realize it but it's the same one from the nursery. Luke 1:45.

"How did I miss this before?" I ask myself out loud. "And blessed is she that believed: for there shall be a performance of those things which were told her from the Lord."

I start to tear up and then I get mad at myself for crying. I pull the journal to my chest and begin to talk to God.

"God, I believe in your word and never will I doubt your power. I don't know what you have in store for us but if you don't mind, please send an extra portion of strength. Cover my husband now as his body is wracking with pain. Do for him what we cannot. And when you see fit to end this storm, I'll be ready. And God, send peace to my mind which overshadows what my natural may think. Amen."

2:32 AM | December 20, 2017

Blog Title: Bed Rest

It's 2:32am and it seems like I am having more mornings like this. Unlike other mornings, I am confined to a bed in the hospital.

It sucks!

I've been here now for six days and in spite of it all, I am grateful because the more the babies stay in, the stronger they will be once they are out.

Anyway, I really don't have much to say. I was up and bored out of my mind and I know it's been almost a month since I've shared anything.

Quick update:

1. The babies are almost four pounds each.
2. Their nursery is done.
3. I wasn't expecting to go into labor, this early but I have to trust God's plan.

4. Keith is still fighting to be here when the babies are born. (He is where they get their strength.)
5. Oh, the interview for Happy Baby finally aired. If you all didn't catch it, I will add a link at the bottom. It ended up more beautiful than I could have ever imagined.

In all, even during the storms of our life, we are still here and that's enough to make me thankful.

And with Christmas being five days away, I am reminded of the sacrifice Mary made as she prepared to birth a Savior. If she could do it, I know I can.

As always, don't forget to mention our name in prayer. It is what gets us through.

Just in case I don't blog again, before the holidays, I pray you each have a Merry Christmas and Happy New Year. And may this season bring you more joy than you can stand.

2:32AM

Until next time,

Char.

Charlotte

I wake up when I hear my phone vibrating. It's a FaceTime call from Keith.

"Babe." I say when his face appears on the screen.

"Hey you."

"I am so happy to see your face. How are you?"

"Today is a better day than yesterday. How are you?"

"I'm still here." I say showing the room. "All is well."

"How are the babies?"

"Dr. Meade says they are holding on. My water is still leaking but she isn't ready to break it completely. I am still getting steroids and

2:32AM

antibiotics to fight off any infections so I am in good hands."

"Good."

"Are you up to coming to see me later?"

"Yes, I will be there."

"Okay. Get your rest and don't try to overdo it. If you can make it, come but if not, stay home and call me."

"Yes ma'am."

I laugh.

"I love you Charlotte."

"I love you too boo."

SOME TIME LATER

I open my eyes to see Keith.

"Hey you." I say stretching. "You came."

"Of course I did. I told you I would."

"What time is it?"

"2:32."

"Keith--" I say sitting up.

"Babe, I tried to wait."

"No, no; where's Virginia? Virginia!"

"Shh," he says sitting on the side of the bed and pulling me into him.

"No, you can't leave. Not now, the babies aren't here yet."

He wipes my tears.

"Please don't go yet. I'm not ready to let you go." I say hitting his chest. "You said you'd be here when the babies were born."

He grabs my arms.

"Please baby, please."

2:32AM

"I wish I could stay. I wish I could take the pain away. I wish a million things but none of them matter now."

"I can't do this without you. It's too hard."

He rocks me.

"God, please not now."

He hold me until my sobbing becomes a whimper.

"Thank you for being one of the best things to ever happen to me. I knew when I met you in freshmen orientation you would be my wife and our life together, far exceeded my expectations. I don't know where I go from here but my spirit is in God's hands. I love you beyond words, Charlotte Renee Hulbert and don't you ever forget it. Use the memories that fill your heart to last you a lifetime."

"But I want you."

"I know but you have to trust God's plan in all of this."

"God's plan is to make me suffer, isn't it? It's not fair. It's not fair!"

"You're hurting but it won't always be like this. One day, you'll understand God's plan. All I ask, don't put your life on hold for me. Yes, you'll mourn but you have a life to live and two babies who will need you and your strength. And when you are ready, give your heart to the man God will send to love you longer than I could."

"Please don't go--"

He holds my face in his hand. "Whenever the pain gets to be too hard, know my suffering ended the moment God called my name to rest. And when you cannot sleep, allow my memories to comfort you. I love you Charlotte and I always will."

He kisses me on the lips and walks out with me screaming his name.

"Charlotte, open your eyes. Charlotte."

I open my eyes to the nurse standing over me and the machine going off.

2:32AM

Just then Dr. Meade comes in.

"Deb, what happen?"

"I don't know, she was screaming in her sleep."

"Charlotte, are you in pain?"

I cry out.

"Deb, the babies' heart rates are dropping. Call upstairs and put them on standby for an emergency C-section."

"Yes ma'am."

"Charlotte, I need you to calm down or we will have to take the babies tonight."

"He's gone," I scream. "My husband is gone."

Dr. Meade pulls me into her and I continue to cry.

"Charlotte, I'm going to give you something to calm you down."

Charlotte

I open my eyes to see my mom and dad sitting next to my bed.

"Hey baby, how are you feeling?"

"He's gone, isn't he?"

She nods her head and I begin to cry again. She comes over to me.

"Charlotte, you've got to calm down."

When I move, I cry out in pain. "My babies?"

"They are fine."

"Did I hurt them? Please tell me I didn't lose them too."

"Charlotte, they are fine. She weighs three pounds, three ounces and he weights three pounds, six ounces. They are in the NICU but they are fine."

2:32AM

I cry even harder.

"Why couldn't God wait? Why did he have to take him now? He was supposed to be here."

"I don't know but it's going to be okay."

"You don't know that! How can it be alright when my husband is dead?"

"Charlotte--"

"Just get out. GET OUT!"

My dad grabs me as I hear a nurse's voice come over the intercom.

"How can I help you?"

"I need a nurse, right away." I hear my mom say. "Please hurry."

"Just leave me alone," I cry.

"Charlotte, please baby." Mom says.

"It hurts. It hurts so much."

When I open my eyes, its night again. I look around the room for Keith. I knew he wouldn't be there but I held out hope to see him again.

I close my eyes as the tears fall. I hear the door open and when I feel somebody's hand on my arm, I open them to see Pastor Lawson.

It makes me cry harder.

"Charlotte, I wish I had the words to take away your pain."

With one hand, he grabs my hand and the other, he covers my forehead.

I continue to cry.

"Father God, I come asking you to incline your ears to your servant because I need you tonight. God, I don't have to go into detail because you already know so I'll only ask for you to strengthen your daughter. She's been through so much this year, oh God, deliver now.

2:32AM

For the days and nights, she'll have to endure, strengthen. For the moments when it feels like she can't go on, hold her up. For the nights she'll cry, comfort and the moments she feels alone or overwhelmed, let her feel your touch. God, we will not question your will but I ask you to cover Charlotte and her babies.

Make stronger their lungs, protect their hearts, give sight to their eyes, hearing to their ears and the flow of blood through every vein. We know you will because your word says all we have to do is ask. Have your way God. Let her rest and in the morning when her eyes open, may her burden feel lighter. Amen."

"We are here for you Charlotte. Whatever you need, me and the entire church body we will be right here for you. You rest now and let us cover you."

Keith Jr. and Kia

Dad wheels me into the NICU to visit my babies. They are in an incubator, side by side with tubes in their nose and little covers over their eyes.

"Hi, I am Nicole, the nurse caring for your sweet babies."

"How are they?"

"Let me get Dr. Mendez for you."

"Hello, I am Dr. Javier Mendez. Are you the parents?"

"I am Charlotte, the mom and this is my dad, Charles."

"It's nice to meet you. You have some strong babies. They both have small nasal cannulas, just to help with their breathing. We will also have them on a peripheral IV line, for the next several days, in order to give them intravenous nutrition and medications. Baby boy has a little jaundice but it is to be expected."

"What about breastfeeding?"

"You can begin to nurse although you may not generate a lot of milk, at first but again, this is to be expected. We will start them to nurse at your breast, in a day or two as we work on getting them to suck, swallow and breathe; while feeding. Please don't get discouraged if they are not able to latch, right away."

"Do you have any idea how long they will stay here?"

"If all continues to go well, I would like to keep them until they are at least five pounds and right now, I don't know how long it will be."

"When can I hold them?"

"In a few days, once we get their body temperatures stable." He says.

"Is there anything else we have to keep a watch on?"

"In about a month, we will examine their eyes."

"Their eyes? Why?"

"Yes. Babies born earlier than thirty-two weeks run the risk of developing premature eye disease, called retinopathy of prematurity or ROP but it is treatable."

I sigh.

"Charlotte, I know this is a lot to take in but they are in great hands and we will do everything in our power to ensure you go home with two healthy babies."

"Thank you Dr. Mendez." My dad says.

When he walks off, I go up closer to them.

"Hey little ones, it's your mom. I am so happy to have finally met you. I wish your dad could have been here to see you but I know he's

2:32AM

proud. You keep being strong so we can break out of here soon. Mommy will be back to see you two on tomorrow. I love you."

"Have you chosen names for them yet?" Nicole asks?

"Yes. Keith Oliver and Kia Grace."

"Beautiful names."

"Thank you. Please take care of them."

"I will."

Charlotte

I've been home now for three days. It was so hard to leave the babies but I know they need to be where they are.

It's been hard to get around, after having an emergency C-section and trying to make arrangements for Keith's funeral. It sounds so surreal to say, Keith's name and funeral, in the same sentence but it is now my reality.

I had to call and break the news to his sister Karen and it broke me to hear her heartbreaking cry.

The funeral home, I selected, has been amazing. They came to the house to help plan the details. They are even able to handle everything, down to the flowers and obituaries.

2:32AM

His service will not be for another two weeks because I cannot imagine trying to stand for any amount of time, right now.

"Baby girl, how are you feeling?"

"Hi daddy. I'm okay. What about you?"

"I cannot complain. What are you working on?"

I sigh. "Keith's obituary."

"Do you need any help?"

"No, I think I have everything. Where's mom?"

"She's in the kitchen, she bought some dinner for you. Have you talked to Keith's sister?"

"Yea. She'll be here in a few days."

"Will his mom be able to make it?"

"No. Unfortunately, her dementia has gotten worse and she has become violent so Karen had to put her into an assisted living facility."

"I am so sorry to hear that."

"Me too. I wonder if she can sense Keith is gone."

"I am sure she can." He says.

"I asked Karen not to tell her about Keith's passing, though."

"Why not?"

"Because it's hard enough dealing with it, when you can remember. Imagine her having to relive it over and over during her lucid moments. I don't know if she will but I didn't want to take the chance."

My phone rings.

"Excuse me daddy."

I answer and put it on speaker.

"Hello."

2:32AM

"Mrs. Charlotte, this is Amanda from Harrison funeral home."

I hear screaming in the background.

"Yes ma'am, is everything okay?"

"Well, there is a lady here who is demanding to see your husband's body."

"Who is it?"

"Her name is Dakota Marshall. I told her she would need your permission--"

"Oh hell no! She does not have my permission to even be in the same room as my husband's body."

"Yes ma'am."

"And if she continues to cause a problem, call the police and have her arrested."

"Yes ma'am and I am sorry to have bothered you."

I release the call.

"Can you believe this, this—I don't even know what to call her!" I slam the phone down.

"What happened?" Mom says coming into the room.

"Dakota is at the funeral home trying to see Keith's body."

"WHAT?" Mom screams. "I knew it was something not right about that girl, in the head. The nerve of that--"

"Ruthie, don't you dare. Charlotte has already told the funeral home not to let her in."

"What's going to stop her from showing up at the funeral and acting a fool?"

"How does she even know where his body is because it hasn't been released yet?"

"You don't think she's watching you, do you?"

"I don't put anything pass her but I am not in the mood for her drama. She can try me if she wants and I can guarantee, it'll be a day she will not forget."

"Okay, calm down Hulk Hogan. You are in no condition to do anything." Dad says.

"Let her try and I'll show you."

"Do you want me to have security at the services?"

"No, I will not allow her to make a spectacle of Keith's memorial."

"Well, let us know what you want us to do and we will. In the meantime, come and eat so you can have your strength to nurse the babies today. We will not let her ruin anything else as it relates to your life." Mom says.

2:32 AM | January 4, 2018

Blog Title: 365 days

It's 2:32am and I am sitting at the island in the kitchen. I have pictures spread across it as I try to find pictures to finalize the video for Keith's Memorial Service.

As much as it hurts, I cannot help but to remember my sweet girl because today would have been Micaela's first birthday.

365 days.

I sometimes find myself, when I am alone, picturing her. I wonder if she'd be walking and saying words or if she'd have Keith's deep dimples or my small ones, when she smiled. I think about the kinds of food she would have eaten. Would she be picky like her daddy or willing to try anything like me?

2:32AM

But death showed up, 239 days ago and stopped time for me. All I have now are the memories and a hole, forever etched in my heart twice the size it was before.

See, death showed up again on December 22 at 3:12am and took with him, my husband. While Keith was slipping out of his old body, I was in surgery delivering our son and daughter.

Life and death.

Things we cannot control.

Now, I have to prepare to say goodnight, again and this time it is even harder than before. I knew it was only a matter of time before Keith left me but I still wasn't prepared.

Can you ever be?

I read this scripture last night that I want to share with somebody who may be going through one, hell of a storm right now. You may not understand it neither can you see how you will ever make it through but I have to believe, for you and me, we will.

Psalm 73:26 says, "My flesh and my heart may fail, but God is the strength of my heart and my portion forever."

So tonight, even though I am grieving, I am not alone because somebody, somewhere is fighting an equally hard battle.

I'm praying your faith will not fail.

Until next time.

Char.

Keith's Wake

January 12, 2018

"And I heard a voice from heaven saying, "Write this: Blessed are the dead who die in the Lord from now on." "Blessed indeed," says the Spirit, "that they may rest from their labors, for their deeds follow them!""

Revelations 14:13

Charles (Charlotte's Dad)

We walk into Temple of Praise.

Charlotte, Karen, me and her mom as we are met by Pastor and Lady Lawson.

"Charlotte, I know these next few days are going to be hard but you have people around you who love you. Lean on us, if you need too."

"Thank you." She says hugging each of them.

"Would you like to be left alone?" Pastor asks her.

"No, please stay."

She holds even tighter to my arm, the closer we get to Keith's casket. She wanted to be the first to see him.

2:32AM

"Jesus!" She screams as soon as she sees his face. I grab her from behind. "I can't. I can't. I can't. Oh God, help me."

I lead her away at the same time Karen lets out a scream.

"My brother! My brother is gone."

Pastor Lawson grabs her right before she passes out. He motions for some ushers to bring a blanket, water and a towel.

"Daddy, this hurts so much."

"I know baby but I'm right here for you."

"When will my storm end? I don't know if I can take much more. Please tell me it'll be over soon."

"Baby girl, I cannot tell you what I don't know for sure. What I do know, without a shadow of a doubt is, it definitely has to end."

She sits, nestle into my arms. Her legs are shaking as she stares at the casket.

"Never would I have imagined my year beginning like this. One minute I am somebody's wife and in the blink of an eye, I'm a widow left to raise two children on my own."

"You are not alone. You have me, your mother and your church family. We all love you and you know if I could carry your burdens, I would."

"I know daddy. Thank you for being here."

"I wouldn't be anywhere else."

We sit there for another ten minutes or so until Charlotte sits up.

"I'm ready now."

I help her to stand. She slowly walks over to the casket and just stands there, rubbing her hands together.

She rubs his face and smiles as the tears fall onto him. Her hands move down to his chest while her head shakes back and forth, like she's saying no.

2:32AM

I rub her back.

She continues to cry

"I miss you so much. There are so many things we did not get to do but I thank you for loving me, Mr. Keith Oliver Hulbert, Sr. and know I will forever cherish your legacy through the parts of you left behind. If you get a chance, kiss our baby girl for me. Rest on until I see you on the other side of the sky."

When she turns back to me, Karen is being escorted in by Ruthie and the pastor.

She's still crying.

"Daddy, I'll be back."

"Will you be okay?"

"Yes, I just need a minute to myself."

Charlotte

Walking out of the sanctuary.

"Charlotte."

"Dakota, what are you doing here? Haven't you done enough?"

"I am not here to cause trouble."

"Then what could you possibly want? Keith is dead."

"Please, hear me out."

"Hear you out? Girl, if you don't get out of here. I am not in the mood for your drama, your fake tears or anything else you have to offer."

"I just want to see him, one last time."

"Bit--"

2:32AM

Before I can say anything, she runs past me into the sanctuary. The ushers try to catch her but she makes it to his casket.

I stand at the door and watch her as she cries and scream his name. It takes daddy and Pastor Lawson to pull her away from the casket but not before she kisses him.

ON.THE.LIPS.

WITH.RED.LIPSTICK.

The morticians have to steady the casket to keep it from falling over, while they drag her to the door.

She's still screaming and causing a scene.

"Wait," I tell them.

"Charl--"

I slap her so hard spit flies from her mouth. I then grab her by the collar of her dress.

"Make this your last time ever being in my presence because if you don't, you'll regret the day you were born. Get her out of here and make sure she cannot get back in."

"You can't do this!" She screams. "I loved him. KEITH! I just wanted to see him! KEITH!"

"Are you okay?" Lady Lawson asks, walking up behind me as they push her out the door.

"Yea, I'm just glad no one else was here to see this mess."

"Me too. This chick is certifiable crazy."

"Yes, she is."

"Do you need me to do anything?"

"Can you have the morticians clean Keith's face while I go to the bathroom?"

"Of course."

I walk into the bathroom and splash some cold water onto my face. Grabbing some paper towels, I look at myself in the mirror.

"Peace Lord, is all I need. Just a moment of peace."

Keith's Memorial

January 13, 2018

"So we are always of good courage. We know that while we are at home in the body we are away from the Lord, for we walk by faith, not by sight. Yes, we are of good courage, and we would rather be away from the body and at home with the Lord."

– 2 Corinthians 5:6-8

"Your tears are just temporary relief. Your tears are just a release of the pain, sorrow, grief. Your tears are expressions that can't be controlled. A little crying out is alright, but after a while you won't have to cry no more; don't you worry, God's gonna wipe every tear away. I won't have to cry no more, when I reach the other shore."

Angela sings.

"Jesus!" My mom yells.

I have my arms wrapped at my waist as I cry from the emptiness of my soul.

Karen hasn't stopped crying. Thank God for Keith's aunt and uncle being here for her.

"You won't have to cry no more."

Angela says as she continues to sing.

When she is done, Pastor Lawson stands to give the eulogy.

"Death shows up and it knocks the wind out of you. It's like being in a boxing ring. In one corner you have life and in the other corner is death. Every time the bell rings, life and death meet in the middle. Unlike actual boxing, there are no rules to say you can't hit below the belt and this is why life can seem unbalanced and sometimes hard to bear.

Those days you survive are the times life keeps knocking the hell out of death. Oh but when God calls and He says, "Final round" or in other words, "Well done servant," it is then death gets the final hit. And while it may be hard, we yet rejoice in knowing Keith was already prepared because His trainer, Jesus, was in His corner telling him how to stand to handle the impact of the blow.

His trainer Jesus, whispered in His ear, it's time and the fight is already fixed in your favor. So, you see, dear brothers and sisters, Keith didn't die on December 22nd; he simply marked the win in his column as heavyweight champion and he bowed out gracefully. Yes, it was hard to see him go but he'd already made preparations.

Yes, it hurts to know you will not see his face again, on earth but let his memories hold you. For after a while, we will not have to cry tears down here anymore because there's a place waiting for us. A place man's hands had no part in building. A place that welcomes us in and never lets us depart."

"Brothers and sisters, Keith gained his belt in glory and if you desire to see him again, all you need is to be on the Lord's side."

The rest of the service is a blur. From the many friends who spoke kind words, the hugs, condolences and sorry for your loss comments; we finally make it to the family car.

Karen is still a wreck. She hasn't stopped crying yet. I reach over and touch her hand but she never stops looking out the window.

We make the fifteen minute drive to the cemetery. When the driver opens the door, I put my shades back on and grab my dad's hand as we are lead to his final resting place.

The weather is unseasonably warm, for January but I take it as God's way of saying, it is well.

"You ready baby girl?" Dad asks.

"No but I don't have a choice."

We make it to our seats as the funeral director passes us red roses, wrapped in blue ribbon.

Angela stands at Keith's casket and belts out the words to "When I See Jesus, Amen."

By the time it's over, my hands are lifted and there is a smile on my face because I know where Keith is.

He's resting until He sees Jesus. Amen.

His pain is gone. Amen.

His suffering is over. Amen.

He gained eternal rest. Amen.

My tears may not be over but it is well.

We are told to stand.

"To you, O Lord, we commend the soul of your dearly beloved servant, Keith Hulbert. Forgive whatever sins he may have committed, on earth and welcome him into your everlasting peace. For we count it all joy to know it has pleased our Heavenly Father, to take unto Himself our beloved son, husband, brother and father. We therefore commit his body to the ground, earth to earth, ashes to ashes, dust to dust, looking for the blessed hope and the glorious appearing of the great God in our Savior Jesus Christ."

"You may now place your flowers."

2:32AM

"It is Jesus who shall change the body of our humiliation into the likeness of His own body of glory according to the working of His mighty power. Let us pray."

Angela begins to quietly sing, "It is well, with my soul. It is well, it is well, with my soul."

"Heavenly father, the creator and sustainer of life; mysterious are your ways toward us. God, right now, at this moment we thank you for life but more than that, we thank you for death because we know, in death you have the power to give us peace. In death, you have the power to ease our pains and troubles. In death, God, you have the power to give us rest.

So God, we thank you. Thank you for the life of Keith and thank you for the legacy you allowed him to leave behind. Now God, comfort this family, don't leave them alone but comfort them when confusion tries to slip in. Hold them in the hours when sleep will not come. Rock them on the day the tears will not stop and remind them they are not alone. In thy hands, God, I commit the spirit of your servant, saying it is well. Amen."

We all say amen.

"We, on behalf of Harrison Funeral Home, thank you for allowing us to serve your family during this most difficult time. We ask in the days, weeks and months to come; when the phone calls and visits stop, you will continue to pray for this family. If there is anything we can do for you now or in the future, please do not hesitate to call. You are now dismissed back to your cars."

Before leaving the cemetery, we wait until they have fully buried Keith's casket before going to Micaela's grave. She is buried right next to her daddy and I could not leave without taking a moment with her.

2:32AM

I know she's not there, spiritually, but her body is. Dad lays his suit jacket down for me, as I kneel at her tombstone.

"Hey sweet girl. Although I know you're not here, I could not pass up the chance to see your tombstone. Daddy told me how pretty it was and now I can see it for myself. Speaking of your daddy, he is resting next to you. I don't know how it is, in eternity but if you get a chance, kiss him for me. I miss you and I will always love you."

I lay the flowers there before my dad helps me up. Walking back to the car, the wind blows across my face.

For a moment I stop.

"It is well." I say.

"Did you say something Pudding?" Dad asks.

"No sir."

Charlotte

When we finally make it home from the repast, I am the kind of tired where you can sleep for several days. Mom, dad, Karen and Angela are here, making a fuss.

"Charlotte, you really haven't eaten much today. You want me to fix you anything?"

"No ma'am, maybe later. Right now, I just want to lay down for a while."

I don't give them the chance to change my mind. I walk into the bedroom and close the door before stripping out of my clothes. I turn on the shower, pin my hair up, remove my makeup and stand under the hot water.

Then I allow my tears to flow.

"God, I'm hurting." I say hitting the wall of the shower. "Please, I just need a touch from you."

2:32AM

"You've got to show up." I whisper. "You've got to show up."

I stand there for a little while longer, not caring my hair is now soaked and I really haven't washed my body.

I drag myself out of the shower and wrap my robe around me, not bothering to dry off or apply lotion.

When I open the door, I see a box on the bed.

I dry my eyes with the sleeve of the robe before walking over to it. Picking up the note, it reads … "I'll always be with you. Keith."

I drop the note and open the box.

"A music box."

Lifting the lid, it begins to play, A Ribbon in the Sky."

There is another note on the inside of it. I sit the music box on the nightstand before pushing the other box out of the way and climbing into the bed.

I take a deep breath and open the note.

"My dearest Charlotte,

Since I will not be there to dance with you on our 20th anniversary, here is a token of remembrance so you never lose your song or your faith again. And whenever life's burdens seem to wear you down or you find yourself missing me, open this box and dance. Because "We can't lose with God on our side. We'll find strength in each tear we cry. From now on it will be you and I and our ribbon in the sky. (Yea, I copied the lyrics. LOL.) I love you Mrs. Charlotte Renee Hulbert. I did on earth and I will in eternity. -- Keith"

When I look up, Karen is in the door.

"Did you do this?"

"I was only responsible for delivering it. Keith set it all up."

"When?"

2:32AM

"When the two of you came to visit me in Cincinnati."

"Thank you. It is exactly what I needed."

"And thank you for loving and forgiving him because it was what he needed. He loved you Charlotte."

"And I loved him too."

I spend the next few weeks getting the house prepared for life with twins. It seems all I do is pump breast milk and eat. It is never-ending but I wouldn't change it for anything.

We celebrated their two month birthday on February 22st, in the hospital with mom and dad.

Did I tell you they have been a present help in my time of need? I don't know what I would have done without them.

The babies stay in the NICU went a little longer but I dare not rush it. If it took six months to get them home, it would not have mattered.

"Hey, you ready?" Nicole asks, bringing me out of my thoughts.

"Yes, I am. Are you two ready to blow this joint." I say to the babies after they have been fastened in their seats.

Kia stretches and KJ burps.

"I'll take that as a yes."

"Let me get a picture." Nicole says handing me a sign that has their release date on it.

March 5, 2018.

Forty-five minutes later, I pull up at home to Mom, dad, Karen, Pastor and Lady Lawson, Angela and her husband standing outside with a sign and balloons.

I pull into the garage and get out.

2:32AM

"What is all this?"

"This is a welcome home baby shower."

"You guys. I said I wasn't going to cry today."

"A little crying never hurt nobody." Mom says.

We get them and all of their things out the car. I didn't realize it but it felt good to have something to celebrate. In fact, it felt really good.

When we were done opening the gifts, I take them out to the memorial garden. They didn't know it but I had Keith's name and dates added to the bench.

Yes, we all cried but they were tears of remembrance and joy.

The next afternoon, I am standing at the door of their nursery when Karen taps me on the shoulder.

"Hey, you okay?"

"Yea, I'm good. What about you?"

"I'm good. I didn't mean to disturb you but Dr. Mitchell is here."

"Okay, I'll be right there."

"You want me to stay with the babies?" She asks.

"No, they are good. Why don't you come and sit with us."

"To talk to a shrink? Nah, I'll pass."

"It may do you some good. At least give it a chance."

"Okay but if I don't like it, I'm leaving."

"Deal."

I walk up to the living room.

"Dr. Mitchell, thank you so much for coming. I know home visits are not part of your program."

2:32AM

"There isn't a program that cannot be changed." She says taking a seat on the couch and pulling out her notebook and pen.

"Dr. Mitchell, this is Karen. She's Keith's baby sister. I asked her to join us."

"It's nice to meet you Karen."

She gives a half smile which Dr. Mitchell notices.

"Charlotte, I know you've been through a lot lately. The last time I saw you, Keith was in the hospital and he has since passed away. How are you coping?"

"Is this a joke?" Karen asks. "How do you think she's coping? She's had to bury her daughter and her husband, not a year apart and you ask how's she coping?"

I start to say something but Dr. Mitchell shakes her head.

"Is this what you get paid to do? Ask stupid questions? Charlotte, are you really going to sit here for this?"

I grab her hand.

"This is stupid, right?" She asks, her voice softening. "How can you cope with so much lost when my heart feels like it is missing most of its pieces? Huh? How are you coping?" She cries.

"Karen," I say unable to stop the tears. "I can cope because I have no other choice. I have some little people depending on me to make it. However, I want you to understand something, this isn't easy because it is, by far, the hardest thing I've ever been through."

"But I've watched you get up every day with your head up and your shoulders back when all I want to do is crawl into the nearest dark corner and cry myself to sleep. You smile when suicide fills my thoughts. I have a sick mother who doesn't even know me and now my brother is gone and if my pain hurts this much, I can't even begin to imagine yours."

"I show you what you need to see, in order for you to make it." I tell her.

"I don't understand." She says.

"If you knew the many nights I wanted to swallow a bottle of pills, you probably wouldn't believe me. If you knew how much time and effort it takes for me to pull myself together, you probably wouldn't believe me. If you knew the many mornings, I've found myself sitting in the floor of the nursery, at 2:32am, willing God to take my life; you probably wouldn't believe me. Baby, there is nothing easy about grief but we can survive it."

"Karen, I am sorry my question upset you but it is these kinds of questions, during this time, that allows your raw emotions to come out. When you can truthfully deal with what's bothering you, the enemy cannot use it against you. This is why I have to ask the hard questions. Do you understand?"

She nods and Dr. Mitchell continues.

"Nobody ever said death is easy and I can bet you, nobody ever will. No matter if it's sudden or expected, death is still death. This is why you have to deal with your feelings instead of bottling them up because the enemy is somewhere close, stalking your every move. And when the time is right, he'll step in to use your fear against you, making you believe you have nothing else to live for."

"She's right." I add. "After losing Micaela, I was so angry at God. I was losing my faith in Him because I couldn't understand why He would give me so much suffering. I felt like He was dangling happiness in my face and when I got close enough to grab it, He'd snatch it away. I would spend many nights, crying out for Him to hear my prayer, only to get silence in return."

"Charlotte, I hear all this but it doesn't make the pain of losing my only brother any easier."

"What does?" Dr. Mitchell asks. "Karen, nothing can make the pain of losing a loved one easier but you can cope with it by dealing with it."

"I'm not ready too." She says.

"And you have every right. I am not here to force you to do anything but don't stay in the darkness too long."

"Thanks for your advice. Please excuse me."

When Karen walks out, I turn back to Dr. Mitchell.

"Charlotte, how are you coping?"

"A breath at a time."

"Do you still feel like you're a shell of a person?"

"In a way I do but I am starting to find my substance again."

"How has it been having the babies' home?"

"It's been hard because I want to watch them every minute just to make sure they are breathing. The first couple of nights, I would sit in the nursery to ensure they made it pass 2:32AM. Is that crazy?"

"No, you been cautious but now you have to be willing to put them in God's hands."

"I am Dr. Mitchell but I am so scared of losing my faith again."

"Charlotte, you do know your faith didn't fail you last time, right?"

I sigh.

"James one, verses two through three says, "Dear brothers and sisters, when troubles come your way, consider it an opportunity for great joy. For you know when your faith is tested, your endurance has a chance to grow. Charlotte, our endurance is tested, every now and then to ensure its keeping power can still sustain."

"Keeping power?"

"When it feels like you are sinking yet you haven't drowned, that's keeping power. When you should be crying but you smile instead, that's keeping power. When you should have lost your mind but didn't, that's keeping power."

"Keeping power." I repeat.

"I'm sorry Charlotte, I didn't mean for our session to go this way but God needs me to remind you of Romans five, verses three through five which tells us, "but we rejoice in our sufferings, knowing that suffering produces endurance, and endurance produces character, and character produces hope and hope does not put us to shame, because God's love has been poured into our hearts through the Holy Spirit who has been given to us.""

She stops talking and gets up, saying over and over, "My God, my God!"

I am rocking back and forth as I feel the Holy Spirit saturating the room. I open my mouth and instead of words, I speak in tongue.

"Oh God, have you way."

I kneel down on the floor and I hear Dr. Mitchell praying.

"God, I am taking you at your word because I know what I heard. I heard you say you'd make our burdens light. Your word says, for our present troubles are small and won't last very long. Yet they produce for us a glory that vastly outweighs them and will last forever! I know what I heard oh God. So we don't look at the troubles we can see now, rather, we fix our gaze on things that cannot be seen. For the things we see now will soon be gone, but the things we cannot see will last forever. That's your word and we take you at your word."

I don't know how long Dr. Mitchell and I stay in worship. All I know is, my living room floor

2:32AM

turned into an altar and I laid out, prostrate before the Lord.

    Willing.

ONE MONTH LATER

I am standing outside, in the backyard at 2:32am, April 10th, 2018. It's been an entire year since I found Micaela in her crib but instead of wallowing in my grief, I decided to have my own memorial for her.

With Keith Jr. and Kia.

Both of them asleep in their stroller.

I light the lantern and lift it towards the sky.

"On this morning, when I want to remember the horrible thoughts of that night, I instead remember you, Micaela Olivia Hulbert. We only got to spend 96 days with you, in flesh but I take joy in knowing we will get to spend eternity in spirit. Rest on my sweet baby girl, until we meet again. We love you."

I release the sky lantern and watch it float away.

2:32AM

I wipe the tears and take the babies' into the house. I put them back in their cribs before sitting in the rocking chair.

I play this song, I recently heard by Tamela Mann, I Can Only Imagine.

I allow her voice to soothe me as the worst year of my life begins to replay like an old movie. I close my eyes and hum with the music.

A year ago, my life was rocked at its core.

A year ago, my life began to tumble towards me, like an avalanche and I couldn't control it.

A year ago, things changed.

I open my eyes.

Yet, here I am.

Watching my double reward sleep, peacefully. So now, instead of counting those days, I count the days of my joy.

From December 22, 2017 until now.

109 days.

2616 hours.

156,960 minutes.

The time it took for me to regain my joy.

Yes, 12/22/17 has dual meanings but I am taking joy in both because Keith also received his reward.

So now, I've found my faith in God again and my testimony is like David's in Psalm 126, verse five; "Those who sow with tears will reap with songs of joy."

It hasn't been easy but I refuse to lose my faith in God again because I'd rather have Him and not need Him than to need Him and not have Him.

2:32 AM | April 15, 2018

Blog Title: A Poem of Remembrance

I know it has been months since I have blogged but life has been moving, swiftly. Some days and nights are still hard as I mourn and raise two babies but I press on.

However, I logged on tonight to share something with you. God woke me up and gave me these words and like before, I am penning them to the blog, so I will not forget them.

I am also sharing it for you, whoever you are who may be going through. Whether it has been three days or three years and your pain is still running deep, I am praying for you to never lose your faith in God.

Here goes...

A Poem of Remembrance

You were taken from us before the sun had a chance to rise. One minute you're asleep, the next moment you died.

We wanted to question God, there must be a reason why. Then God whispered to me, before she was yours, she was mine.

I countered, but God I need answers because this pain runs deep. He simply said, hush child and rest, I'll speak when you sleep.

So I closed my eyes and waited, I needed Him to appear. He did but it wasn't to explain, it was to let me know He was near.

He showed me your face and how peaceful you look, then I realized why your life, He so easily took.

2:32AM

    You were too good for this mean world, your time here was done. God sent angels to get you, to bring you into His arms.

    I hated to see you leave but I understand it better, it seems. And this is why I take comfort in your memories and seeing you in my dreams.

    Rest well little one.

    Signed,

    A Grieving Mommy.

Thank you for taking the time to read 2:32AM. I pray it has helped you to see every storm we endure, has a purpose.

You may not be dealing with the loss of a child but maybe it is the loss of a loved one or even a relationship.

Whatever it is, grieve it but do not lose faith in God.

Trust Him.

"For after you have suffered for a little while, the God of all grace, who called you to His eternal glory in Christ, will Himself perfect, confirm, strengthen and establish you." – 1 Peter 5:10

2:32AM

Can I pray for you?

Our Father in Heaven,

For the person reading this prayer who may be weary in body and spirit, it is they I need you to touch. The person who cannot stop the tears, the nightmares, the night sweats and anxiety attacks. The person who keeps looking for their morning joy because their weeping has gone on too long.

For the family who is grieving, the mother who had to bury a child, the child who had to bury a parent and the sibling who had to close the casket on a brother/sister; help today. Blow fresh winds of peace from every direction, on those who need to feel you.

Even if their battle isn't over and they have to suffer a little while longer, let them know their sacrifice isn't in vain. Help today God for they shall not be defeated neither will they give up because victory has to be theirs.

Amen.

If you are wondering if the journal Charlotte mentions is real, it is. It is titled, HEROINE ADDICT: Journaling your way to becoming addicted to the heroine you are.

Why is this journal different from all the rest? It was created in the hope you will become addicted to heroine. No, not the drug but the woman you are and destined to become. The woman who is admired by others, who is held in high regard and who is favorable and filled with courage.

You can order a copy through this link:

https://www.paypal.me/AuthorLakisha/15

About the author

Lakisha Johnson, native Memphian and author of ten titles was born to write. She'll tell you, "Writing didn't find me, it's was engraved in my spirit during creation." Along with being an author, she is an ordained minister, co-pastor, wife, mother and the product of a large family.

She is an avid blogger at kishasdailydevotional.com and social media poster where she utilizes her gifts to encourage others to tap into their God given talents. She won't claim to be the best at what she does nor does she have all the answers, she is simply grateful to be used by God.

Again, I thank you for taking the time to read my work! I cannot express what it means to me every time you support me! For upcoming contests and give-a-ways, I invite you to like my Facebook page, AuthorLakisha, follow my blog authorlakishajohnson.com or join my reading group Twins Write 2.

If this is your first time reading my work, please slide over to Amazon and check out the many other books available:

A Secret Worth Keeping
A Secret Worth Keeping: Deleted Scenes
A Secret Worth Keeping 2
Ms. Nice Nasty
Ms. Nice Nasty: Cam's Confession
Ms. Nice Nasty 2
Sorority Ties
The Family That Lies
Dear God: Hear My Prayer
The Pastor's Admin
The Forgotten Wife

Doses of Devotion
You Only Live Once
Heroine Addict – Women's Journal

Connect with Lakisha:

Facebook: KishaDJohnson | AuthorLakisha

Facebook Group: Twins Write 2

Twitter: @ _kishajohnson

Instagram: kishajohnson

Snapchat: Authorlakisha

Email: authorlakisha@gmail.com

Amazon by searching Lakisha Johnson

Made in the USA
Middletown, DE
23 February 2019